18 Hours to Us

KRISTA NOORMAN

BOOKS by KRISTA NOORMAN

The Truth About Drew
Goodbye, Magnolia
Hello, Forever
Until Then
18 Hours To Us

For Chloe.
My gymnast.

1
All His Fault

I *hate yellow cars.*

These were the words that crossed Natalie's mind that Saturday in early May as a glimpse of yellow bumper peeked out from behind the trees at the crossroad ahead. The bright morning sun glared off its windshield as it came into full view and stopped, but she didn't need to see inside to know who was sitting behind the wheel.

Colton Daynes.

You couldn't miss him in that shiny yellow Chevy Camaro with the black stripes that his daddy bought him when he turned sixteen. Colton, with his honey-brown hair and stunning green eyes and a body like one of those statues on display in a piazza in Italy. Not that she'd ever been. Italy was the vacation of her dreams. And Colton's presence had graced more than a few of her dreams as well.

As Natalie rapidly approached in her little grey Honda Accord, the yellow car inched forward from its place to her left. Only, it kept moving.

He's not actually pulling out right now, is he?

The wheels of Colton's Camaro suddenly squealed as he made a go of it, turning out in front of her. Panic shot through her body, and she gripped tightly to the steering wheel. If he had gone just five seconds sooner and if she had been driving just a little slower, she might have had time to stop properly. Instead, she was forced to swerve right to avoid him. She stomped on the brake, glancing in her rearview mirror at the car traveling not so far behind. Her biggest concern in that instant was not whether that car would hit her or even if she would

1

Colton and Dad moved her suitcase and bags from the trunk of her car into the Camaro.

Natalie gave her dad a quick hug, but as she pulled away, he locked his arms tightly around her. "Daddy, I'm fine."

"I love you," he said.

She turned her head and placed a kiss on his stubbly cheek. "I love you too."

"Call me if you don't catch the bus." He kissed the top of her head.

"I will." She turned from her dad's arms and found Colton holding the door of his car open for her.

"Do you need any help?" He extended an arm to her.

"You should be really thankful that I don't." She brushed past him, anxious to get to the school, and climbed into the last car in the world she ever thought she'd be riding in. Her body sank into the comfy leather seat—black with yellow stitching—and she caught a whiff of Colton's cologne, or maybe it was that new car smell she had always heard about. She wouldn't know. Her car was fifteen years old, and her dad had never had a car younger than ten years old.

Colton took his place behind the wheel and looked over at her.

She gave him a weak smile, and he drove away slowly.

Natalie noticed the time on his dashboard read 9:12 a.m. "I don't think we're going to make it."

As they rounded a curve and were out of sight of the accident, his foot pressed harder on the accelerator. "Think again."

Natalie glanced over at the speedometer as the needle passed eighty miles per hour. "I thought you didn't speed."

"I never said that. I've just never been caught." He winked at her.

She rolled her eyes.

A notification went off on Colton's phone, and he reached for it.

Natalie snatched it before he could.

"Hey!" he exclaimed.

"Seriously? I've already come close to death once today. I'm not going to die because you can't wait five minutes for a text."

"Read it to me then."

His lock screen was a picture of his girlfriend, Lexi—pretty, blonde, cheerleader, popular. But *mean* was the adjective Natalie would use to describe her, and she had the Snapchat screenshots to prove it.

"Passcode?" she asked.

"8008." He snickered.

Oh my word. He's such a child.

She opened his phone to another shot of Lexi—this time in a skimpy bikini. Natalie wished she had Lexi's confidence. Colton would never notice her when he had a girlfriend who looked like that. It wasn't like she couldn't wear a bikini if she wanted. She had been a gymnast since she was six, so she was fit and in shape. But they were on a different scale when it came to looks. Lexi and Colton were the pretty people. Pretty people always went for other pretty people. Not that Natalie wasn't pretty in her own way. She had long, smooth brown hair, which she kind of loved, and pale blue eyes. Her beauty was simple and natural. She was happy in a t-shirt and jeans and the ratty o.d. green military jacket she had stolen from her dad. Not the kind of thing Colton would go for. She wasn't popular. She wasn't a cheerleader. She wasn't Colton's type.

"It's from G-Dollar Sign."

Colton laughed. "G-Money," he corrected her.

"It says 'OKC, where u at? Bus is rollin.'" She had no idea what OKC meant, and she wasn't sure she wanted to know.

An expletive left Colton's mouth, and he pushed the accelerator harder.

Natalie clung tightly to the door. "Colton! Slow down!"

He had to, whether he wanted to or not, because they had to turn left onto the road that led to the school.

When they arrived twenty minutes late, the parking lot was empty. Natalie's stomach sank.

Another text chimed on Colton's phone. She glanced down to see it was from G-$ again just before Colton took his phone back. It read "Sorry, man. See ya when we get back."

More expletives. Colton got out of his car, slammed the door, and paced around for several minutes.

Natalie fought back tears of disappointment and annoyance at Colton for ruining this for her. She pulled out her phone, about to text her dad to let him know they missed the bus, when Colton opened the door and bent down to look at her.

"Maybe we can catch them." There was a glimmer of hope in his eyes.

"Catch them? They've got, like, a twenty-minute lead on us."

"So."

"Well, if we did catch them, what would you do with your car?"

"I can get you to the buses and drive the rest of the way by myself."

She shook her head, which made the throbbing worse. "You can't drive that far alone. What if you fall asleep and crash your car and die?"

He thought for a few moments, then nodded. "So, let's just do it."

"Do what?"

"Let's drive there ourselves. You can be my copilot."

"I don't know." A case of nerves took over in her stomach, and her mind raced to all the reasons she couldn't go. "All the money I brought is for when I get to the beach. I don't have extra for gas or food for a road trip."

"I'll pay. It's my fault we're in this mess anyway."

"That's true."

He gave her an amused look.

She simply stared at him, not sure how to answer.

"What do you say?" His eyes pleaded with her to say yes.

"You aren't a very safe driver, Colton. My parents would never allow it." *Dad.* The biggest and most important reason to say no.

"You're eighteen, right?"

Natalie nodded.

"Well, then you can do whatever you want."

She looked as uncertain as a beginner skydiver about to take a leap for the first time.

"They don't have to know you didn't catch the bus," he said.

Her mouth fell open and a little huff escaped. "You want me to lie to my parents?"

"Do whatever you want. I'm going. With or without you." He walked to the back of the car, leaving the door ajar, and started talking on his phone to someone.

Natalie's head was pounding. She couldn't think straight. She grabbed her purse and rifled through the contents until she found her bottle of ibuprofen and popped a few, hoping it would take the edge off the pain.

She stared out the window at nothing in particular. Could she do this? Could she really take this trip with Colton? She brought up Google Maps on her phone and typed in Virginia Beach. From their high school in the little village of Middleville, Michigan, it was a thirteen-hour drive.

Part of her was terrified at the idea of riding another minute in a car with Colton. The other part got a thrill just thinking about spending hours alone with the guy she'd had a crush on since she was six years old.

Her phone chimed then with a text from her best friend, Olivia, asking where she was.

Colton climbed back into the car and looked at her. "What do you say?"

She had never done anything crazy like this. Ever.

"You in?" He raised an eyebrow at her.

Natalie took a deep breath. "I'm in."

She peeked out from under the shirt. "Maybe I should just call my parents and tell them what happened."

Colton started the engine and cranked up the volume on his premium sound system. He gave her a conniving grin. "I'm sorry. I didn't hear you. The radio was too loud."

"Maybe you should take me home." She tried to speak above the music, but he turned it up louder as he took off down the road.

"What was that? I can't hear you." He laughed, clearly thinking himself clever.

Natalie reached over and turned the volume all the way down.

His eyes widened, and his mouth fell open. "Hey! Hands off my radio."

"You are ridiculous."

"And you're a chicken."

Her mouth fell open this time.

"Why does it matter if those girls saw us?" He looked back and forth between her and the road several times, waiting for her answer.

"I don't want to get into trouble." She exhaled an exasperated breath. "Things just aren't going according to plan."

"You always have a plan, don't you?"

"Most of the time." Actually, all of the time, but she didn't want to sound like some kind of control freak. "This was supposed to be a fun trip with my best friends."

"It'll still be fun. I mean, have you met me?"

She rolled her eyes. "Yes, I realize you're the life of the party."

"No, I mean, seriously ... have you met me? Because I don't remember ever meeting you."

Funny guy. "We've met."

"I think I would've remembered." His tone smooth and flirtatious.

"Apparently not."

"You do look kind of familiar," he told her. "At least give me a hint."

She thought back to first grade, climbing on the jungle gym together, holding hands on the bus. He had told her she was his girlfriend and that one day he was going to marry her. But they were six. He couldn't possibly remember that. Or that he'd broken her tiny little heart when he got a new fiancée at recess the following week.

Their only other contact was a few classes they had shared over the years. But they hadn't really spoken since that elementary school proposal, so it was no wonder he didn't remember who she was.

"You don't know me, Colton." Her head hung a little. "You never have."

He quieted for a few minutes of silent driving.

She was very close to asking him to drive her home, when he finally spoke again.

"Tell me one thing about yourself, one thing you love."

That's easy. "Gymnastics."

Colton's eyes lit up as if he had solved a piece of the puzzle. "Oh, right. You're the gymnast."

Her brow furrowed. "What does that mean?"

"Nothing." He smirked.

She was about to ask again when her phone signaled a text—another message from Olivia along with two she had missed.

Livvy:
Are you OK?
Why aren't you on this bus?
Why aren't you responding?

Natty:
Got in an accident this morning.
I'm OK, but I missed the bus.

Livvy:
Obviously.
Glad you're OK.
So, what? You're not coming?

Natalie paused with her thumbs over the screen. Stay or go? She made a quick mental list of pros and cons. Asking Colton to drive her home, missing out on the trip, and forfeiting all the money paid went under one column, while risking life and limb to get to Virginia Beach and going behind her dad's back to do it occupied the other.

The safe choice versus the choice Dad would surely see as immature and irresponsible. A wave of nausea hit her at the thought of lying to her father. Or was it from the whiplash?

She peeked over at Colton and chewed on her bottom lip. He was staring ahead, tapping his hand against the steering wheel, bouncing his knee to the beat of the music, oblivious to the battle that was raging inside her mind.

Livvy:
Hello?

                    Natty:
Yeah, I'm coming. Getting a ride.

Livvy:
With who?

                    Natty:
Colton Daynes.

Her phone rang immediately.

"Hey, Liv," she answered.

"Colton Daynes?" Olivia shrieked. "Did I read that right?"

"*Shhh*! Yes." Natalie glanced over at Colton, who had obviously heard because he was smirking again.

"Are you with him right now?"

"Yes."

"In my dream car?" Olivia was in love with Colton's car, even more than most girls were in love with its driver.

"Yes."

"How did this happen?" Olivia asked.

"Hang up, and I'll text you."

"Oh, right. You can't talk because he's sitting right next to you. I get it." She was all giggles.

"Right."

"This is crazy. You do realize that, don't you?"

"I know." Natalie was very aware of how unexpected and unbelievable this situation was.

"Lexi's going to flip."

Lexi. Why hadn't she thought about how Colton's girlfriend would react to them traveling together? Her name should've topped the cons side of the list.

"Please, don't say a word," Natalie begged. "To anyone."

"I won't."

"Good."

"I'm gonna go so you can text me. Livvy out."

"Na ... out." Normally she would've said "Natty out," but she didn't want to give Colton any clues to her identity. Leaving him in the dark was way too much fun.

As soon as they hung up, Olivia started in again with the texts. Natalie barely had a chance to tell the story without being interrupted with a hundred questions. When she had finished telling Olivia the events of the morning, she glanced over at Colton then back at her phone.

Natty:
Where are you right now?
Maybe we can still catch up to you.

Livvy:
What? You mean you don't want to ride with him?

Natty:
I don't know.

Livvy:
Have fun! And I want to hear every detail when we get there.

Natty:
OK.

Livvy:
Livvy, out.

Natalie tucked her phone into her purse and stared at the road ahead.

"Who's Liv?" Colton asked.

Crap. "My best friend."

"It's one of the Olivias then." He looked pleased with himself for finding another clue. "Is it Olivia Strauss?"

"No."

"Olivia Benton?"

"No." She glanced over at him then back at the road.

"Olivia Fenmore?"

Double crap. She paused before her reply. "No."

"Ha! It is! You suck at lying."

She rolled her eyes. "You remember all of *their* names, but you don't remember mine?"

Colton appeared to be deep in thought for a moment. "Olivia's best friend is Trinity Collins."

"Yes, Trinity is our other best friend."

"I didn't know they had another best friend."

"That's because I don't go to parties with them," she replied. "I'm usually training."

"For gymnastics?"

"Yes." She was proud of how hard she worked at the sport she loved.

"You should come to more parties."

"Why?"

"Because you're missing out."

Her laugh came out as more of a snort. "What, on a bunch of underaged drunks making idiots of themselves? I'm good."

"You *are* good, aren't you?" He seemed to be sizing her up.

She looked over at him. "So what if I am."

"Good is boring," he declared.

"Gee, thanks." The second-guessing began again.

"I'm not saying you're boring. I don't even know you ... I'm sorry, what was your name again?"

She tried not to smile. "Nice try."

"I will get it out of you. The road is long, and my will is strong." He raised a fist in the air as if to demonstrate that strength, and Natalie's eyes locked on his bicep.

Look at the road. Look at the trees. Look at the dead raccoon on the side of the road.

"Oh my gosh, you're a poet." She was surprised she could form a coherent sentence. "You're just full of hidden talents, aren't you?"

"And I've got the queen of sarcasm in my car. This oughta be fun."

"I can be fun."

Colton laughed out loud. "Oh, I bet you're loads of fun."

"You'll never find out now. I've decided to be boring for the rest of the trip, just for you."

Colton looked over at her and smiled, a glint in his vibrant green eyes. "I look forward to a very boring trip then."

And her sarcasm melted away.

"Want some ice cream?" They had traveled maybe thirty miles when Colton veered off of the road into the parking lot of MooVille Creamery.

Natalie glanced at the clock on the dash. "We haven't even been on the road for an hour and you want to stop already?"

"This place is my favorite. And did I mention ice cream?"

She shook her head in disbelief. "If we stop every time you want ice cream, we'll never get there."

"So, you don't want any?" He climbed out of the car.

"I didn't say that." She followed him toward the entrance, past the picnic tables and benches, and into the large white building with the cartoonish cow logo above the door.

"Hey, Colton," the woman behind the counter greeted him. "Do you want your usual?"

"You bet," he replied with a smile. "What do you want?" he asked Natalie.

She perused the menu. "Small chocolate shake is fine."

Colton shook his head at her. "Boring."

"Colton," she warned. If he kept saying flirty things like that, she might give in to her urge to flirt right back.

He patted her on the arm. "I'm just messin' with ya."

"Well, don't."

"All right. Don't get your panties in a bunch."

Natalie grimaced. "I hate it when people say that."

"Well, calm your butt then."

"Oh my gosh." She turned on her heel and headed toward the car. He caught up to her as she dropped her cup in the trash.

"Lighten up … you."

A giggle escaped. It was fun keeping her name from him. She wondered if she could keep it up for the entire trip.

Her phone dinged in her pocket, and she pulled it out and stopped in her tracks at the text.

"What? Who is it?"

"It's my dad." Her heart rate accelerated.

"What'd he say?"

"He asked if I made it to the bus." She had never lied to her dad before, and she didn't want to start now.

"Just tell him you did."

"I can't." Her throat constricted. "I can't lie to him."

Colton leaned back against the passenger side of his car. "It's not too late to go back. If that's what you want, I'll take you home."

She didn't want to go home. Every part of her wanted to go on this trip … with Colton.

"But just so you know …" His eyes locked with hers. "I really want to go on this trip with you."

His smile made her forget all the reasons she shouldn't go. Her mind whirled with the options.

After standing frozen to that spot for several long minutes, she finally typed a message back to her dad and tucked her phone in her pocket. "OK. Let's go."

Colton opened her door for her, and she climbed in.

When he was back in his seat and all buckled in, he turned to look at her. "I have to ask. What did you say?"

"I told him we're on our way to Virginia Beach."

3
Names

It was a partial truth. A little white lie. But it was more than that and she knew it, because she didn't keep things from her dad. She never had. They had always been open and honest with each other, especially after her mother left them, when Dad was all she had to get her through those all-important early teen years. Twelve was too young to be without a mother, but Dad had done a pretty great job of making sure she knew she was loved, that his shoulder was there to cry on, his arms always open when she needed a hug, and that her faith in God would sustain her through it all. It had been just the two of them for three years, until Norma came on the scene.

Ever since her dad remarried, things had been different. Much of his free time was spent with Norma now, and the bond they once shared sometimes seemed like a distant memory. Maybe it was because she was all grown up and didn't have to rely on her dad so much anymore. But she still wanted to. She wanted to cling to him and the times they had shared together. He had always been her best friend, and she missed that. She missed him. And she secretly envied the time he spent with his new wife.

If Dad found out she had lied to him, it would surely cause more distance between them. Lying was the one thing her father did not condone after all the lies Mom had told him. She knew it, yet she'd done it anyway. And she didn't know if he would forgive her for it or not.

The text tone on Colton's phone brought her out of her thoughts, and he motioned for her to read it.

"G-Money again. He wants to know if you're bailing on the trip."

Another tone chimed. "And one from Sexy Lexi." She could barely get the name out without gagging. "She says she will never forgive you for ditching her, and you better write her back right now or you're through."

Colton rolled his eyes.

"Do you want me to respond to these for you?"

"Tell Grant I'm on my way."

"Grant is G-Money, I assume."

"Yeah."

"What about Sexy Lexi?" She said the name in the best valley girl voice she could conjure up.

Colton smiled, revealing his perfect pearly whites. "I'll text her later."

Another string of texts came in from Lexi, and Natalie read them aloud.

Sexy Lexi:
```
Baby, I don't want to do this trip without you.
I miss you already.
Where are you?
The bus is so lonely.
What happened?
```

She read the messages to Colton. "I probably shouldn't be reading these."

"Tell her I'll see her in Virginia Beach."

Natalie did as he asked, but it wasn't the end of Lexi's messages.

Sexy Lexi:
```
Yay! Are you driving there?
Who's with you?
If you're alone, be careful.
Don't fall asleep at the wheel and crash
and damage that hot bod of yours.
```

"I can't handle many more of these," Natalie admitted.

"Just turn the ringer off for now."

She clicked the switch on the side and flipped his phone screen-side down.

"Sorry. She can be a bit much sometimes."

"I know. We used to be friends."

"You and Lexi?" He said it like it was the most outlandish thing he had ever heard in his entire life.

"Yeah, a very long time ago."

"When?"

"Until seventh grade when she got boobs and boyfriends and I didn't. Apparently, that made her too cool for the likes of me."

Colton nodded. "Sounds like her."

"What do you see in her?" The words slipped out of her mouth before she could stop them.

"You mean besides the obvious?" he replied with a twinkle in his eye.

She found no humor in his response. "Are you really so shallow?"

"What if I am?"

Natalie shrugged her shoulders. "I guess it just confirms what I already thought about you."

"Which is?"

"You and your friends live to party and date only the prettiest and easiest girls in school."

His eyes were fixed on the road, and he gave no reply.

"You don't take life or your relationships seriously. And you couldn't care less about school or your future."

"Now, hold on. You've got it all wrong."

"Oh, do I?"

"I would do anything for my friends. Ask any of them. I would drop whatever I'm doing and be there if they needed me. And they would do the same." His volume level had risen. "We're more like brothers at this point." He looked pointedly at her then back at the road. "And I care about my future. I've got a football scholarship—"

"To MSU." Natalie finished his sentence. "Yeah, I know. Everybody knows."

"So don't lump all of us together like one great big stereotype," he insisted.

She raised her hands in surrender. "All right. I'm sorry."

4
Remembering

Natalie!"

She jumped awake with a start. "What? What is it?" Her eyes darted to the road in front of them.

Colton's palm smacked the steering wheel. "Natalie! Ha! You're Natalie Rhodes." He seemed extremely pleased with himself. "Gah! That's been driving me crazy for the last hour."

She rubbed her eyes. "Congratulations."

He glanced over at her. "It's all coming back to me now."

"I'm happy for you."

"We were engaged once, you know."

Natalie's mouth dropped open a little. "Is that so?" She played it off like she didn't know what he was talking about so she could see how much he actually remembered.

"Oh, yeah. I think we were five, maybe six. We climbed up that jungle gym on the playground, and I told you I wanted to marry you."

Natalie laid the back of her hand against her forehead and faked a swoon. "So romantic."

He gazed in her direction, those hypnotic green eyes reflecting the sunlight outside. "You were my very first girlfriend, you know."

Her stomach fluttered at the look in his eyes, but she pushed it aside. "And I obviously made a lasting impression on you."

He nodded. "Hey, at least one of us remembered that very romantic proposal."

She chuckled, but still didn't let him know that she remembered. That she had never forgotten.

"You snore, by the way."

Natalie looked at him, her mouth agape. "No, I do not."

He laughed. "Uh, yeah, you do."

She wiped at her mouth, realizing she may have drooled a little in her sleep.

"It's a cute snore. Like this little muffled breathing sound. Kind of like a puppy."

"You're comparing me to a dog?" Her icy blue eyes widened.

"It's a compliment, Natalie."

Her name on his lips caused a warmth to spread over her.

Natalie looked out the window as they drove past fields of newly planted corn. "Where are we?"

"Ohio somewhere."

They passed by a sign for I-90 East. "Wait, are we on the turnpike?"

"Yeah."

"No! We were supposed to keep going south. That's the route the bus is taking!"

"I followed the GPS, and this is the way it took me. It's the fastest route."

Natalie searched for the email the school had sent about the trip. "The hotel where the bus is stopping is in Charleston, West Virginia."

"So, put it in the GPS."

Natalie fiddled with the screen until she was able to enter the address of the hotel.

"Recalculating," the device said. "You will arrive at your destination at 5:52 P.M."

Colton activated his blinker and exited the highway. "In the meantime."

"Where are you going now?" Natalie was annoyed that Colton seemed to do whatever he wanted and go wherever he wanted without so much as considering her. But since he was paying for this little road trip, she didn't feel like she should complain.

"I have to pee." He paid at the toll booth and headed to the nearest gas station.

She too felt the urge as soon as he pulled in.

"Will you top off the gas for me?" he asked as he climbed out.

Natalie exited the vehicle and watched him swipe his credit card at the pump. "You're not the only one who has to go, ya know."

"You can't hold it for two minutes?" He was practically hopping up and down.

"Fine. Go." She waved him away and tried not to laugh as he sprinted across the parking lot.

She rounded the car and began pumping the gas. Through the driver side window, Natalie noticed Colton's phone light up with a new text. She opened the door and looked at his screen.

Sexy Lexi:
I'm missing your kisses right now.

She groaned and went back to watching the numbers on the gas pump rise.

"Your turn," Colton called from across the parking lot.

As he strolled up, she stepped right to move around him, only he moved in the same direction. She stepped left, but he moved too.

"I didn't know you could dance." He chuckled.

A nervous laugh escaped her as she attempted another step, but Colton stopped her with a gentle grip on her upper arms and rotated them ninety degrees so she could pass. She looked up into his eyes, and he gave her a slight smile—enough to reveal the dimple in his right cheek—before releasing her.

Her pulse danced and her arms tingled from his touch, but she checked herself. *Get a grip.* She walked on toward the building, glancing back over her shoulder to see if he was watching her, which he was.

"You have another text from your girlfriend, by the way."

"Great." There was nothing but sarcasm in his tone.

She thought about his response the whole time she was in the restroom. Shouldn't he be happier to hear from his girlfriend? Were there problems between them? That certainly wasn't the impression she got from Lexi's texts.

When she returned, Colton was in the driver's seat again.

"Still not going to let me drive?" she asked as she buckled in.

"I'm not tired yet." He pulled out onto the road and turned right, passing by the highway on-ramp.

"Why aren't you getting back on the highway?" Natalie pointed at the GPS.

"I'm starving, and I know a great restaurant right on the water."

"On the water?" They were nowhere near a lake. "How far out of the way is it?"

"Not far." He winked.

Why did she not believe him?

"Or what?"

"Or ..."

"Cole?" A tall handsome man with the same honey-brown hair as Colton walked toward them with a huge smile on his face. He appeared to be in his mid-to-late-thirties and was dressed in a blue polo shirt and khaki pants like some of the staff she had seen waiting on tables.

Colton and the man met in a hug, patting each other on the back. "It's good to see you, Neil."

"You too. What are you doing here?" He looked over Colton's shoulder at Natalie. "I thought you were on your way to Virginia Beach."

"We are. Long story."

Neil's head bobbed in a nod. "OK. Well, let's get you fed."

Colton motioned for Natalie to join them. "This is my friend, Natalie, from school."

She held in a laugh. They had never been friends.

"Very nice to meet you, Natalie. I'm Colton's cousin, Neil." He shook her hand.

"Nice to meet you too."

Neil led them to a table upstairs on the deck overlooking the marina. "Missy will be over in a minute to take your order, and I will be right back." He took off down the stairs and a waitress showed up seconds later with menus and took their drink order.

"Get anything you want," Colton told her as they perused their menus.

"Oh, I will." She grinned at him. "So, we came to see your cousin?"

"Yeah. And free food."

Natalie's eyebrows scrunched up in confusion.

"Neil owns this place," Colton explained.

"Oh, that's cool. So, you've been to this area a lot then?"

"We have family here, and my parents are members of the yacht club."

This didn't surprise her in the least, but she still fought the urge to roll her eyes, knowing he was Richie Rich.

The waitress returned with their drinks, took their meal order, then left them again.

"The yacht club, huh?" Natalie wondered what that kind of life was like.

"Yeah, we spend summers at the club and out on the boat."

"Sounds wonderful." She envisioned the warm sun on her face, the splash of the water as the boat cut through the surface, Colton at the helm.

"I guess." He shrugged his shoulders.

Imagining herself with Colton was nothing new, but she'd never done it with him sitting mere inches from her. She took a sip of pop and filed her crazy fantasy away with the rest of them. "Don't they have a restaurant at the club?"

"Yes." Colton rolled his eyes. "This place is more my style."

This surprised her. Despite his nice car, nice clothes, and unlimited cash flow, he'd rather be at this simple bar and grille than at the yacht club with his own kind.

"You don't like spending summers there?" She wanted to know more.

"My parents are more into status and their social calendar than anything to do with me. I was left on my own a lot."

"So, you hung out with Neil?"

Colton nodded. "Yeah, Neil and his wife, Heather, live not too far from here. I used to hang out at their place a lot and help out here when they were first getting it up and running. They've always been good to me. Especially after ..."

She noticed his eyes go soft and sad as his words trailed off. "After what?"

"Uh ... after, well ..." He seemed to scramble to find words. "Just whenever I needed them."

He looked pained, and she had the urge to comfort him. "It's nice to have close family like that to get you through hard times."

"Yeah."

She wondered what had happened, but she didn't want to pry. He obviously didn't want to talk about it, especially to someone he barely knew.

Neil returned then, grabbed a chair from a nearby table, and pulled it up to the end of theirs. "So, tell me why you aren't on the bus with your class."

Colton and Natalie exchanged glances, then Colton filled Neil in on the events of the day.

"How're you feeling, Natalie?" Neil asked after Colton's story came to an end. "A collision like that can cause a lot of aches and pains. Not to mention a concussion."

She turned her head side to side, and her neck still felt stiff. "I'm a little achy, but I took some ibuprofen. I'm all right."

"You didn't mention that." Colton immediately appeared concerned.

"It's no big deal, Colton."

"If you feel sick at all, you have to tell me, Nat." He reached across the table and touched her hand. "OK?"

She could barely respond as the butterflies took off in her stomach, flitting this way and that. His hand was warm on hers, and she hoped he hadn't noticed all the hairs on her arm standing up. It took a few extra seconds to register that he had called her Nat. When people called her that, it reminded her of the pesky bugs. Definitely not her favorite nickname. But when Colton called her Nat, it somehow had a different ring to it.

"OK?" he repeated.

"I will. But honestly, I'm fine." It wasn't the whole truth, but she didn't want to worry him unnecessarily.

Colton let go of her hand as the waitress returned with their meals.

"If you two need a place to stay for the night, you know you're always welcome to stay with us," Neil told them.

"Thanks, Neil, but we're trying to catch up with the bus so Natalie can get back to her friends."

"All right, well, I'll leave you to it then." Neil stood and returned the chair to its original table. "Come and say goodbye before you head out."

"We will," Colton replied.

Neil departed, and they dug into their meals. Natalie tried not to devour her chicken sandwich and fries like an animal, but she was so hungry. Colton must've been feeling the same because neither of them spoke while they ate.

Colton took the last bite of his burger and patted his stomach. "So good."

Natalie nodded as she set her napkin on her empty plate. "I feel so much better now." She washed down her food with the last few sips of her pop, then opened the camera on her phone and snapped a picture of the harbor and marina. She pointed her phone at Colton, and he held out his hand to block his face.

"Nah, you don't want a picture of me."

"Seriously? The king of selfies doesn't want his picture taken."

Colton's eyes fixed on hers, his expression turning deathly serious. "Why'd you call me that?"

"I don't know. Because you're always posting selfies with Lexi and your friends. Everyone in the school knows that."

"Just don't call me that, OK?"

Natalie's stomach turned a little at the thought of upsetting him or offending him in some way. "All right. Can I ask why?"

"No," he snapped. He wiped his mouth with his napkin and wadded it up, standing abruptly and heading for the stairs.

Natalie said nothing more, only followed him downstairs to say their goodbyes to Neil.

"I hope you'll come back again, Natalie." Neil gave her a friendly handshake.

"I'd like that." She looked over at Colton, who still seemed upset.

"Have you thought any more about this summer, Cole?" Neil asked.

"I haven't decided yet."

"We'd love it if you came. We need an answer soon, so think about it seriously."

Colton nodded. "Thanks for lunch."

Natalie wondered why he didn't seem to want to answer Neil's question, but she wasn't about to ask him now.

"Anytime." Neil turned to Natalie. "Don't let him drive through the night." He gave Colton a warning look. "You let her drive some too, Cole."

Colton grumbled under his breath.

"Promise me." He pulled Colton into a hug.

Neil seemed more like a dad to Colton than a cousin, and Natalie wondered if that was part of why Colton came there, because he didn't have a great relationship with his dad.

Colton hugged him loosely, and Natalie heard Neil quietly tell him to be careful.

"I will."

"Have a good trip." Neil gave a friendly wave and went back to work.

Despite whatever she had said to tick him off, Colton still opened the doors for Natalie.

She stopped by her open car door. "Are you sure you don't want me to drive?"

When he stood there without a reply, she climbed in, hoping the rest of the trip wouldn't be as awkward as it felt at that moment.

6
Regret

Natalie stared out the window at the lovely lake houses, wondering why her use of the phrase *king of selfies* had upset Colton so much. She wanted to broach the subject and apologize, but she wasn't sure what she would be apologizing for. If she could go back to the restaurant and take back what she had said, she most definitely would. This silence was absolute torture.

Natalie's phone chimed, and she was relieved to see a text from Olivia.

Livvy:
Where are you now?

She typed a quick reply letting her know they had stopped for lunch.

Olivia wrote again.

Livvy:
Lexi is fuming. She's mad that Colton won't answer her texts. I think she hates not knowing what happened. I so want to go tell her and rub it in her face.

Natalie typed as fast as she could.

Natty:
Do NOT do that.

Livvy:
I would never. But it's tempting, right?

Natalie looked over at Colton. His eyes were fixed on the road. His phone was going off again too.

"Do you want me to get that for you?" she asked.

He shook his head.

"It's from Lexi."

He shrugged.

"You don't seem to care very much about your girlfriend."

"I care." He finally broke the silence.

"I can write her back for you. I don't mind." That was a lie. She did mind. She minded that he was dating Lexi, because he could do way better than her. Besides the fact that she was beautiful and leggy and put out, she wasn't a nice person. She used to be. But middle school had changed her from the sweet friend she had grown up with to someone she didn't recognize—someone selfish and bossy and rude to just about everyone in the school who didn't do what she wanted them to do.

"*I* mind," he snapped.

"What is wrong with you?"

"Nothing."

"That's a lie. You were fine when we got to the restaurant. I'm sorry if what I said offended you. I didn't mean anything by it."

His eyes were sad again. "I know."

"I know we don't know each other very well, but I'm a good listener. If you need somebody to talk to—"

"I don't." He turned the radio up louder.

Natalie reached for the volume button, and he grabbed her wrist.

Her eyes met his, and she saw a warning there.

She lowered her hand to her lap. This was such a huge mistake. She wished she understood what it was that had set him off like this, because up until now she had been enjoying the trip with him. Very much. But now she wished he would let her out so she could catch a bus or something. Even hitchhiking would be better than the cold shoulder he was giving her.

She opened Snapchat and spent some time browsing through her friends' stories. At least she had something to do to pass the time since Colton wouldn't talk to her.

When she came to Olivia's story, a lump formed in her throat at a picture of her and Trinity posing by the bus that morning with a few of their classmates.

Trinity's story featured a video. "On the bus, heading to VIRGINIA BEACH!" she hollered into the camera, then turned her phone around and showed a view of the students on the bus cheering and waving at her phone. The camera rotated around to Trinity again, and Olivia came into view.

"Without our Natalie." Olivia pouted. "Natty, we miss you so much."

Tears burned behind her eyes as she typed a message to Olivia.

Natty:
Wish I was on the bus with you right now.

Livvy:
What's happening?

Natty:
Colton is a jerk.

Livvy:
Not surprised. Are you?

Natty:
I was hoping I was wrong.

1
The Falls

Another hour in Ohio passed when Natalie saw a sign for Brandy-wine Falls in the Cuyahoga Valley National Park. "Hey, we should check that out."

Colton said nothing.

"Maybe stretch our legs for a bit." She looked at him questioningly. "You shouldn't be the only one who gets to decide where we stop."

He stared at the road ahead.

"Colton, get off at this exit!" She'd had it with the silent treatment.

He jumped at her sudden outburst. "Fine!"

Colton drove the ten minutes to Brandywine Falls without another word and got out of the car.

Natalie watched as he stood there stretching. He didn't bother to open her door this time. She climbed out and took a deep breath, immediately feeling refreshed. She brushed past him on her way to the trail, bumping his arm harder than she meant to.

"Hey!"

She walked on without a word, hearing his footsteps behind her.

They walked in silence along the boardwalk path. Natalie's steps slowed as she took in the beauty of the trees around them, the squirrels climbing and dodging back and forth along the forest floor. She pulled her phone out and stopped to take a picture, not realizing Colton was walking so close behind.

He ran straight into her causing her phone to drop onto the boards at her feet.

"No!" She scrambled for it and crouched down to see the damage. The hairline spiderweb cracks across the surface made her cringe. "Crap!"

"Oh man, I'm really sorry, Nat."

She waved him off. "It was my fault."

"I'll get you a new one."

"You'll get me a new phone?" Her eyebrow raised.

He nodded.

"That's crazy talk. You don't buy something like that for someone you barely know."

"No big deal." He shrugged.

"It *is* a big deal." Surely, he was joking.

"*I* broke it. I should replace it."

"You're serious."

"Why wouldn't I be?"

"Well, thanks for the offer, but I'm good. The phone still works, and I'm sure the screen can be replaced."

He shrugged his shoulders again and walked on.

Accepting something so expensive from him felt very wrong. But she wondered what it would feel like to be able to toss money around like that with little to no thought.

Natalie watched him walk away, admiring him from a distance as she always had. With his tall stature, broad shoulders, and muscular physique, he was made to play football. She turned her phone to silent and snapped a picture of him walking along the boardwalk as it stretched out ahead, surrounded by towering trees. A part of her wanted to share it on Snapchat, but she wouldn't. It was just for her. Besides, she didn't want to start anything with Lexi.

They strolled along the boardwalk that wound around rough, jagged rock formations until they saw the falls ahead.

"Oh, it's so pretty," Natalie gushed.

"Very." Colton looked back at her and smiled for the first time since lunch.

They made their way down the stairs to the observation deck across from the falls, both of them taking pictures as the water poured over the rocks to the creek bed below.

Colton let out a deep breath. "This was a good idea."

She smiled at him, relieved he felt that way.

He smiled back and walked over to her. Putting his arm around her, he maneuvered so their backs were to the falls and held his phone up in front of them.

"See, I was right about the selfies." She immediately snapped her lips together, afraid she had said something wrong again.

He nodded. "You were." He leaned into her, resting his head against the top of hers.

She leaned her head into his shoulder and smiled at his phone as he took a few shots of them. The moment he removed his arm from around her, she missed it.

Colton tapped a few times on his screen.

"You're not going to share that, are you?" she asked.

"Already did." He turned to face the falls again.

"What?" Her pulse quickened.

"Shared it on my story."

"Are you serious?" She opened Snapchat. Sure enough, there was an update from Colton with the picture of them in front of the waterfall. It *was* a cute picture of them. She fought back a smile as she took a screenshot, then gave him a disapproving look. "You shouldn't have done that."

His eyes shifted to her for a moment then back at the cascading water. "What's the big deal?"

"Your girlfriend and the rest of the school," she replied.

"What about 'em?"

"I've had enough trouble with Lexi in the past. I really don't need any more right now."

He looked at her curiously. "What kind of trouble?"

"Don't worry about it."

He faced her head on. "Natalie, what?"

She hesitated. "I told you we used to be friends, but what I didn't say was that she made seventh and eighth grades hell for me."

"How?"

"Pranks. Mean texts. Threats. Anything she could think of to humiliate me, she did it."

Colton's mouth dropped open.

"I eventually found ways to stay out from under her radar, and I had a good support system in Olivia and Trinity and my dad. So, yeah, I got through it. But I don't want anything to do with her anymore, and—" Her phone started going off right then with messages from Lexi and her two best friends, both named Hannah, calling her every variety of name they could think of. She held it up for Colton to see. "I'm pretty sure you just opened up that can of worms for me again."

His eyes widened. "Sorry. I didn't know." He pulled her into an unexpected hug, which took her breath away.

It was over too soon—his arms around her. She gazed up at him as he let go. He looked legitimately sorry and, in that moment, she felt like he really did care about her.

Colton's phone went off with messages from Lexi as well. He hesitantly turned the screen to show Natalie the long string of messages, one after the other, demanding an explanation for why he was with Nasty Natalie.

"I told you." Natalie had grown and changed and matured since middle school, but it was obvious that Lexi was still the same girl she had been back then. Mostly, she felt sorry for Lexi now, but part of her feared the repercussions of Colton's post.

Colton dialed Lexi's number, and she answered immediately.

Natalie could hear her screeching voice going on and on, not giving him a chance to speak.

"Lex!" He rolled his eyes as she babbled. "Alexis, let me speak!" There was silence for a few moments while he waited for her to stop. "We got in a car accident this morning and missed the bus. The accident was my fault so I owed it to Natalie to get her there." He stopped and listened. "No." Another pause. "Stop. Right now. Stop talking. I want you to hear me when I say this ... are you listening?" He paused. "Good. Leave Natalie alone. She did nothing wrong, and she doesn't deserve this. You and your friends stop texting her or we're going to have a bigger problem." Another pause. "Do you understand what I'm saying?"

A blush crept over Natalie's cheeks. He was defending her. To Lexi. And it felt really really good.

"We're going to try to catch up with the buses tonight at the hotel, so I'll probably see you in a few hours."

A little niggling feeling hit Natalie in the gut. Only a few more hours with Colton. Only a few more hours together.

"I'm hanging up now." He hit "end" and tucked his phone back into his pocket. "Sorry about that. Let me know if they bother you anymore."

"You didn't have to do that." But she was grateful that he had.

"Yeah, I did." His mouth curved up in an apologetic smile.

"Thanks."

Colton walked over and leaned against the railing. "I'm sorry about earlier. You just ... hit a nerve."

"I could tell," she said. "And whatever that was about, I'm sorry."

He was quiet for several long moments before he wandered over to a bench and took a seat.

Natalie joined him, and they stared at the falls, listening to the crashing of the water against the rocks, watching a few visitors come and go.

Colton opened his mouth several times as if he was going to say something, then closed it again when he didn't.

"I don't know if you remember my brother," he finally said.

Natalie's heart skipped a beat. Everyone knew about Chris Daynes, Colton's younger brother. The entire community had been shocked when three years ago, at the age of thirteen, he took his own life. Was this why Colton was upset? Something to do with his brother?

Her mouth went dry. "I didn't really know him."

"He was my best friend and a way better person than I'll ever be."

She had an overwhelming urge to wrap her arms around him, to comfort him. "I'm sure you miss him a lot."

"Every day." He stared at the waterfall.

Natalie didn't know what else to say, so she simply sat with him, hoping he would open up to her. The minutes crawled by without a word spoken until seven of them had passed.

"It was my fault, you know."

The words that broke his silence broke her heart.

"No, it wasn't, Colton. You can't blame yourself."

"Yes, I can, because I'm the reason he killed himself."

8
The King of Everything

atalie was speechless. Her heart was in her throat.

"Chris kind of kept to himself most of the time," Colton told her. He didn't have a lot of friends, besides me. Not like I did."

Natalie watched Colton as he spoke, wringing his hands and bouncing his right leg nervously.

"He, uh ..." Colton cleared his throat, maybe to hide how choked up he was getting. "Well, he wasn't good at sports like I was. He wasn't good in school with his grades like I am. Dad was constantly comparing us, making him feel worthless."

"That doesn't mean you're the reason." She wanted more than anything to convince him.

"When he ... " Colton stopped, his chin quivering.

"You don't have to talk about it if you don't want to." Natalie laid her hand on his arm, and he grabbed hold and sandwiched it between his large hands.

"He left a letter ... explaining ... and one thing he said was that he couldn't live up to 'the greatness that was Colton, the king of everything'."

Natalie's shoulders sank. It was her use of *king* that had triggered this. "Colton, I'm so sorry." She could tell he was trying to hold in the tears.

"So, yeah, that's why I freaked out earlier." He took a deep breath in and let it out. "I haven't let myself think about his letter for a while now, and it just kind of hit me, I guess."

"Thank you for telling me."

He nodded, and a tear escaped down his cheek.

She wanted to reach up and brush the tear away. "I can't imagine what you went through and how hard it must still be."

He chewed on his bottom lip. "Some days I don't know what I'm doing any of this for. Most days I just want to stop."

Natalie's heartbeat picked up pace. "Wait, you don't mean stop, like the way your brother did?"

"No." He squeezed her hand that was still nestled between his. "I mean football and the scholarship. Knowing all my successes made him feel so bad about himself makes me not want to do it anymore."

"I'm sure there was more to it than that, Colton. Deeper reasons within your brother's mind that made him feel the way he did. Maybe even chemical imbalances. Sometimes people are broken inside, and they just want to stop hurting. But it's *not* your fault. And you can't stop living because your brother made that choice."

His head dropped, and warm tears dripped onto her hand. She leaned her head against his shoulder, and he let go and turned into her, wrapping his arms around her shoulders. She circled her arms around his waist and held on while he cried into her neck. This was definitely not something she expected to happen on this trip, but if she could help him, it would all be worth it for this moment.

When the tears finally subsided, he loosened his grip and leaned back to look at her. "How do you know so much about this?"

"My mom is clinically depressed." Most of the time, she avoided talking about it, but he had been so open with her, she felt she owed it to him. And maybe sharing some of her story would help him. "She's been in and out of hospitals for as long as I can remember. Since I was a little girl."

He took her hand again, as if to comfort her this time.

"So, I'm no stranger to the damage depression can do. It's the reason my mom left us, the reason my parents divorced … the reason she tried to kill herself. And it took me years to understand and come to terms with it. And to stop thinking it was my fault." She gazed over at the falls. "It never gets easier, though."

"So that wasn't your mom at the car today?"

"Stepmom," she replied.

They sat in silence, holding hands, listening to the sounds of nature.

It wasn't easy to talk about her mom or let any of the memories back in. Dad had always told her it was best to focus on the future and not dwell on the past. But as she thought back to the years after her mother had left, those years when Lexi had made middle school so rough for her, she remembered the depression and anxiety she had experienced, and it made her wonder. Could her mother's condition be hereditary? Could she have some of those same inclinations?

She took in a deep breath as Colton squeezed her hand.

"That sucks about your mom."

She nodded. "That sucks about your brother."

"I've never told anyone about Chris's letter before."

Her heart warmed at his admission. "I'm glad you told me."

"So am I," he replied with a smile.

It felt natural to be sitting there holding hands with him, like they were meant to be there at that moment in time. Natalie was calmer than she'd been in a long time, especially after the stress of gymnastics Nationals.

Colton exhaled and let go of her hand. He stood and walked over to the railing, looking down at the rough terrain that sloped toward the creek. "We should climb down there and get closer to the falls."

Natalie's eyes widened. "What? No way!" She pointed at the signs warning not to leave the marked paths and observation deck.

He glanced over at her with a devious smile.

"Too dangerous," she warned.

But it was too late. Colton was already climbing over the railing and dropping onto the hillside below.

"Colton, come on."

"What're you so worried about? You're a gymnast. Can't you just do some kind of jumps and flips and land down there on that rock."

Natalie giggled. "I'm a gymnast, not a ninja."

"Climb on up there and show me what you've got." He smiled up at her.

"Sure. I'll get right on that."

"Please." He stuck his full bottom lip out and gave her a pout that melted her resolve.

Natalie glanced around and noticed the people who had been there a few minutes before had headed back up the trail, and they were now alone. She laid her hands on the flat top of the wooden railing and shook her head. *What am I doing? Coach Joe would kill me if he found out I was doing this.*

"Nat-a-lie, Nat-a-lie," Colton began chanting.

And up she jumped.

9
Stupid Choices

atalie raised herself up as if mounting a balance beam. She walked forward and did a little of her routine, expertly turning, pointing her toes the best she could in Chuck Taylor's, her arms moving gracefully along with her to keep her balance. If only she had taken a few ibuprofen with lunch, her neck wouldn't be feeling so stiff at the moment. She focused on the falls ahead, knowing she shouldn't be doing this after the trauma she'd experienced, but she arched backward anyway, hands coming into contact with the railing, body moving effortlessly in a perfect back walkover. She closed her eyes, hoping it would mask the pain.

"Go, Nat!" Colton cheered.

Natalie tried not to smile, keeping her focus on balance and tuning everything else out as she had been taught, but it felt really good to have Colton cheering her on. She stepped back and took a breath before a switch leap and split jump combination, landing solidly back on the rail. Her neck muscles spasmed on impact, and she swallowed down a groan.

"You make that look so easy." Colton didn't seem to notice her reaction.

"I've been competing since I was six, so it's taken years to make it look like that."

"Whoa! Twelve years? Impressive."

"I pretty much eat, sleep, and breathe gymnastics." She crouched to jump down.

"What else you got?"

A dull throb had returned to Natalie's head, but she stood again and glanced behind her at the railing, similar in width to a balance beam—maybe even an inch or two wider. She took a deep breath and held her hands up above her head. Her neck twitched again, but she couldn't lose face. Swinging her arms down with the bending of her knees, she threw them back over her head and pushed off the railing, arching her body then pulling her knees close in a back tuck. She extended her legs to meet the railing again, and pain shot through her neck, disorienting her for a moment. The rail was also a bit wobbly for such an impact, and Natalie teetered toward the edge, flailing her arms in an attempt to right herself. *Graceful* was the word on her mind as she lost balance and fell sideways toward the creek.

Colton moved at lightning speed, his arms shooting out to catch her, the weight of her body knocking him backwards into the brush, weeds, and rocks below. He groaned on contact.

"Are you OK?" She propped herself up a little from her position sprawled across his body.

He reached up and brushed her hair back. "Are you?" He sat up a little, putting their faces inches from each other, her body firmly planted in his lap.

Natalie could feel his heart beating through his shirt.

His hand moved over her shoulder, along her arm, over her hip and thigh as he examined to see if she was hurt. "You're bleeding."

She looked down at his hand on her knee and saw what he had discovered—a rip in her jeans and some scrapes from the rough landing. "It doesn't hurt. Just a little scratch." Her head and neck hurt worse than that did.

Colton shifted to get up and groaned again.

"You should let me check you." She climbed off of his lap and onto her knees next to him. "Turn."

He turned his body toward the creek, and she immediately saw red seeping through the fabric.

Hesitantly, she grabbed the bottom edge of his t-shirt and lifted it up.

He peered over his shoulder at her, his eyebrow raised. "Like what you see?"

She softly slapped his shoulder. "I'm trying to see why you're bleeding."

He chuckled and faced the creek again.

She lifted the shirt more to reveal a long cut under his left shoulder blade. "You must've landed on a branch or a rock or something. We need to get this cleaned up."

"Yours too." He stood and held his hands out to her. "I think there's a first aid kit in the car."

She grabbed hold and let him help her, losing her balance and leaning into him.

There was real concern in his eyes. "You sure you feel OK? You've been through a lot today."

"I feel fine." Another lie.

He squeezed her hands, then the two of them climbed up to the deck and made their way back to the car.

Colton popped his trunk and rifled around inside until he found the first aid kit. He opened the passenger door, and Natalie sat down sideways in the seat and rolled up her pant leg. She *was* feeling woozy, but she didn't want to worry Colton with it.

"No blood on the leather," he teased.

He crouched down next to the passenger side of the car with alcohol wipes and antibiotic ointment in hand. "Give me your leg."

"I can do it, Colton."

"It was my fault you got hurt." The concern had returned to his eyes.

"I'm the one who climbed up there, so I have only myself to blame. Besides ..." She waved her hands in front of his face. "I still have the use of these."

"I asked you to do it, so let me help you."

"Fine," she replied reluctantly.

Colton tenderly took her leg in his hands. They were warm against her skin, and the butterflies took off in her stomach.

She slowly breathed in through her nose, trying to ignore the way her body reacted to his touch. She was sure it was one-sided, that being this close to her had no effect on him, but she couldn't help but wonder what it would be like to be in his arms, to be his, to kiss him and hold him and ...

The alcohol wipe rubbing over her scratches caused a quick intake of air between gritted teeth.

He pulled it away and looked into her eyes before continuing.

"Thank y—" She started to speak just as he leaned close and blew on her knee. Goosebumps covered her skin everywhere, and she knew there was no hiding them.

His eyes met hers again, and the corner of his mouth turned up a little.

She swallowed hard and attempted a weak smile.

He squeezed a little antibiotic ointment onto his finger and rubbed it over her scratches, his other hand gently holding her calf.

She couldn't take much more of this torture. It was a relief when he finally covered it with a bandage, straightened the leg of her jeans, and let go. But then things became worse as he stood and grabbed the bottom hem of his shirt, lifting it up over his head. She could've sworn her heart stopped beating, and she had to remind herself to breathe.

"My turn." He faced away from her.

She stood slowly and moved the first aid kit to the hood of the car. The wound on Colton's back was no longer bleeding, but it was red and crusted over. She took an alcohol wipe and began to clean the area.

Colton winced.

"Sorry."

"Do what you gotta do."

A wave of dizziness suddenly hit her, and she gripped his side with her left hand as she worked to clean the cut with her right.

"I like that," he said.

"The sting of the alcohol?" she asked.

"Your hand." He rotated slightly at the waist and glanced down to where she was holding his side.

"Turn," she commanded. "I'm not through with you."

Colton chuckled.

She finished her mission and applied a small amount of ointment before searching for a bandage to cover it. "Maybe you need stitches. It's not bleeding anymore, but it's kind of a gash. You could end up with a nasty scar."

Colton reached for the butterfly bandages. "Just use a couple of these. It'll be fine. A reminder of our trip."

"Men." She rolled her eyes and applied the bandages.

He turned to her then. "Done?"

She glanced at his chest before averting her eyes to the tree line. "Yes. Are you gonna put a shirt on now?"

"Do you want me to?" The soft tone of his voice sent chills up her spine.

"Yes."

"How come?"

She noticed the amused smirk on his face.

"No shirt. No shoes. No service."

His eyebrow lifted.

Her cheeks warmed, and she stared at the ground. "We'll be hungry again soon. Restaurants won't serve us if you aren't wearing a shirt," she clarified.

Out of the corner of her eye, she saw him smile. He shook his head and walked to the back of the car again. He returned wearing a fresh, unbloodied shirt in a deep green that brought out the color of his eyes.

"Better?" He tugged at the bottom hem of his shirt.

"Better."

Colton tossed Natalie the keys. "Your turn."

"Seriously? You actually trust me to drive?" She circled to the driver side.

"Just don't crash." He winked as he disappeared into the car.

She took her place behind the steering wheel, adjusting the seat and mirrors. A wave of excitement came over her followed by a strong wave of dizziness. She really needed those ibuprofen right about now.

"You ready?" he asked.

She breathed in deep and let it out. "Ready."

Colton's car was awesome to drive. Smooth and sleek. She felt special that he allowed her behind the wheel, and she wondered if he had ever let Lexi or any of his friends drive. She pushed the thought out of her mind and took a quick glimpse at him as he slept. He looked peaceful and oh-so-handsome. She fought the urge to reach out and brush a wave of hair off his forehead. And that jawline—that perfectly cut jawline with a hint of stubble forming. Natalie sighed. She wasn't the kind of girl to refer to guys as hot, but Colton really was.

Ahead on the highway, Natalie noticed the signs for I-77, which would lead her south to Charleston, West Virginia, where the caravan of buses were stopping for the night. She also saw signs for I-76 going east into Pennsylvania, the original route Colton had put them on.

A million thoughts raced through her mind. What if she took I-76 instead of merging onto I-77? This trip was nothing like she had expected it to be so far, and although part of her wanted to meet up with her friends, the other part wanted her trip with Colton to continue. Just the two of them.

She passed another sign. Only a mile to decide. What would Colton think when he woke up and discovered that she had turned? What would it mean, if anything, for them? She was sure his flirtation was just the way he treated all the other girls in school, that she wasn't as special to him as he was actually making her feel. But what if she was wrong? What if he was feeling even a fraction of what she was feeling for him? Could there be something between the two of them? Something real?

The green highway signs stared her down as she sped toward them. 77 or 76? Sensible or stupid?

She glanced over at Colton, then activated her turn signal.

Stupid.

10
Talent

Colton had teased her about snoring, but he was doing that very thing, which she found rather adorable. It was exactly the kind of snore people teased about. Loud and steady. She touched his arm, and he immediately stirred, rubbing his eyes like a cute little baby waking from a long night's sleep.

He peered out the window. "Where are we?"

"Still in Ohio."

"Will this state ever end?" His voice was deeper than normal with a slightly scratchy, just-woke-up sound to it.

She felt suddenly flushed. "Are you hungry? Because I'm hungry."

"I think you're always hungry."

"True." She noticed a sign for a restaurant called Italiano Grille. "Do you like Italian?"

"Who doesn't like Italian?" He kissed his fingertips and tossed them in the air like an Italian chef.

Natalie giggled. "Some people don't."

He shook his head. "I don't know a single person who doesn't like Italian."

"My stepmom doesn't."

"I don't know your stepmom."

"I'm just saying, there are people who don't." She activated the blinker at the next exit and caught Colton in her peripheral vision as he sat up straight, arched his back in a stretch, then ran his fingers through his hair.

She gripped the steering wheel and forced herself to watch the road. It was all she could do to keep her eyes off of him. Somehow, he was even more attractive after a nap.

"Favorite Italian dish?" he asked.

"Chicken parmesan."

"So, you're a marinara girl then?"

"You're not?"

"A girl? I think it's pretty obvious."

She gave him a look. "You're an Alfredo guy then?"

"Fettuccini, please."

She smiled as she turned right at the intersection and spotted the sign for the restaurant.

Colton retrieved his phone and groaned.

"What?"

"You'd think she can't function without me, I swear."

"Well, she *is* your girlfriend. She's probably just worried about you."

He shook his head. "She's not worried about me. She's worried about *us*." He motioned between the two of them.

"She couldn't care less about me."

"That's not what I mean."

"Oh." Lexi wasn't worried about her boyfriend's safety. She was worried that he and Natalie were going to hook up while they were together. "Well, that's ridiculous. She has nothing to worry about. Right?"

Their eyes locked for an instant. "Right," he replied.

She drove into the parking lot of the Italiano Grille while Colton tapped away on his phone, reading his messages, she assumed.

The moment she pulled into a parking space, he pointed at the GPS. "Is that right?"

"Yeah."

"You missed the exit for 77."

Natalie stared at the steering wheel, her heart picking up pace. "No, I didn't."

"You did. You were supposed to take 77 about twenty minutes south of the falls." He touched the screen, bringing up the full map, showing her the route they were supposed to have taken.

She watched without a word until he finally noticed the smile she was trying to hide.

A smile crept over his face. "Wow!"

"What?"

He poked her playfully in the arm. "You're sneaky."

"I don't know what you mean." She could barely keep a straight face.

"You went this way on purpose."

She shrugged her shoulders. "Did I?"

"You're having fun with me. Admit it."

"I never said that." A blush colored her cheeks.

"You didn't have to." He laughed. "You're glad you crashed your car and we're on this trip together."

"Well, I wouldn't go that far."

He shook his head, clearly amused.

"Are you mad?" she asked.

"Heck no."

"You're not upset we aren't catching the buses tonight?"

He looked at her seriously. "I'm having fun with you too, Natalie."

She smiled at him, and the smile she received in return reached all the way up to his vivid green eyes.

He clapped his hands together. "Let's eat!"

Italiano Grille was quaint with photographs of the famous sites of Italy gracing every wall. It wasn't a typical Italian restaurant like others she had been to, though. This one had a small stage to one side where some sort of talent show was going on.

The hostess saw them to a seat not too far from the stage, and they listened to a man singing an Italian opera song.

Natalie's eyes grew big as the man hit a couple high notes. She looked over at Colton, who was pretending to mouth the words as the man sang. "Stop." She swatted at his arm. Giggles took over as he continued. "He's going to see you."

Thankfully, the man's song came to a close before Colton's antics were discovered, and the room filled with applause.

The waitress came to take their order as another man took the stage and stepped up to the microphone. "Thank you, Paolo. Next up, we have a local favorite, the one and only Deb, featuring her good friend Davey."

A petite brunette woman with short curly hair and poofy eighties-style bangs stepped onto the stage and took a seat on a small stool. She carried a ventriloquist dummy with red hair and a red shirt and propped him up on her knee.

"It's wonderful to be back at Italiano Grille tonight," she said. "We love coming here."

"I don't," Davey piped in.

"You don't?" Deb asked. "Why not, Davey?"

"It's the food," he replied.

"What's the matter with the food?"

"I can never decide what to eat. It's all so good."

"How do you know, Davey? You have no taste buds."

A few audience members chuckled. Colton rolled his eyes.

The waitress arrived soon after with their order, and a goofy expression settled on Natalie's face at the plate piled high with spaghetti and chicken and lots of marinara sauce. It was a good thing she was at the gym five days a week conditioning because she had a voracious appetite. She heard the click of a camera and saw Colton taking a picture of her.

"Seriously?"

"The way you're looking at that food just screamed to be captured."

"Whatever. Don't post that."

"I won't." He grinned knowingly.

Natalie tried to pretend his grin didn't affect her in any way and took a bite of her dinner.

"Good?" He was still watching her.

"*Mhmm.*"

Colton dug into his fettuccini Alfredo, and they ate in silence, listening to the ventriloquist's act.

"See that table there in the front row?" Davey asked, nodding his head toward an older couple seated next to the stage.

"Yes, I do," Deb replied.

"I think I know him."

"You know the guy?" Deb asked.

Davey shook his head. "No, the table."

Deb looked at Davey curiously. "What do you mean?"

"I think we were made from the same tree." Davey cackled.

A few chuckles were heard over the clinking of silverware against plates as people enjoyed their meals.

Colton sucked a noodle up as he shook his head. "They call this talent?"

"Be nice." Natalie twisted a few long strings of spaghetti around her fork.

The dummy spoke again. "All these candles on the tables are making me nervous."

"Why, Davey? Because you're made of wood?"

"No, because of all the hairspray you use."

Colton rolled his eyes at Natalie. "Oh my gosh."

"It's cute."

"It's lame." He took a drink of water.

"I'd like to see you get up there." Natalie nodded toward the stage.

"No way would I ever be a ventriloquist."

"I mean, just get up there and ... talent."

"You first. You could flip around the stage. But don't fall off the edge because I'm not catching you this time."

"You're funny ... hey, I know, how about standup comedy?" She teased, nodding enthusiastically.

He shook his head.

"What other talents do you have?" she asked.

"None."

"You lie."

"I can throw a football."

"If I remember correctly, you wrote me a poem once."

He tilted his head to the side and smirked at her. "So, you do remember our first grade love affair?"

She hoped the lighting in the restaurant was dim enough to mask her blush.

"Well, I don't think 'Roses are Red' really counts as poetry," he told her.

"I thought it was good for a six-year-old."

"Now who's the comedian?"

"I think I still have it somewhere." She knew exactly where it was, but she wasn't going to tell him that.

"No, you do not."

She nodded and took a bite of garlic bread.

"Do you remember what it said?"

"Nah." She waved him off, even though she remembered it word for word.

He examined her closely as she took another bite of bread. "You do, don't you?"

"I'm eating," she mumbled between bites.

He left it alone, but kept his eyes on her as she ate.

"Stop watching me."

"Where do you put it all?"

"My dad says my stomach is a bottomless pit."

"That seems like an accurate statement."

"Gee, thanks."

When the ventriloquist finished, she went from table to table, handing out her business cards.

"Thank you for coming," she said when she reached Natalie and Colton's table. "Davey and I are happy to do parties and events."

"*She* is, anyway," Davey piped in. "But if it was your party, pretty lady, I would be more than happy."

Natalie giggled.

Colton stared blankly.

Natalie took the business card Deb handed her. "Thank you. Bye, Davey."

"Bye, pretty lady."

Natalie examined the card. Turning it over in her hand, she found a scratch-n-sniff sticker with Davey's picture on it. "I might regret this." She hesitantly scratched the sticker and raised it to her nose. "Pizza," she said with relief and handed it to Colton, who tucked it under the bread basket without taking a whiff.

The announcer from earlier took the stage again. "Now we'll open up the stage to anyone with a talent they would like to share with us."

"Your turn," Colton stated.

"No way."

"I'll get up there and talent, as you say, if you do a little gymnastics routine for everyone."

"Not happening." After her fall earlier, she knew she shouldn't be doing any gymnastics until she let her body recuperate from the accident. But Colton didn't know that. He thought she was fine, because that's what she had told him. At least she'd been able to pop a couple ibuprofen while Colton was sleeping in the car.

Colton took the last bite of his pasta and jumped up from his seat. "We've got talent!"

"All right!" the man pointed to Colton. "What is your name, young man?"

"My name is Colton, and this is my good friend, Natalie." He pulled Natalie's chair out as he passed by.

"Colton." She covered her face with her hands.

"What's your talent?" the man asked.

"Natalie is a gymnast and would like to share some of her floor routine with everyone." He took her hand and tugged her up from the chair, turning her to face the stage, nudging her forward.

"I can't believe you're doing this to me," she muttered under her breath.

The audience began to clap as Natalie and Colton took the stage.

"I don't have my music with me," she whispered.

Colton took out his phone. "What should I play?"

She thought for a moment. "Play the theme song from the movie *Goonies*."

"Seriously?" Colton replied.

"Just search for '*Goonies* Floor Routine Music' on YouTube."

He did as she asked and found it.

Natalie moved to the side of the stage and crossed her arms over her chest, her head tilted to the side, one leg bent across in front of her other. The music began, and she kicked her foot to the side, her arms coming down and gracefully moving along with her body as she rotated. It wasn't her current floor routine music, but she had used it when she was younger. She did her best to make it work with her current routine, dancing across the stage to the other side and turning to prepare for her first run. She knew she couldn't perform all of the skills she normally would because of the lack of space and no safety mats—not to mention her stiff neck—but she did a roundoff back handspring, then continued on with her 360-degree turn. She squeezed her eyes shut for a moment when she came out of the turn, feeling a little dizzy. All eyes were on her as she did a switch leap and split jump combination, then went for one more roundoff back handspring. When she landed, the audience cheered, but the room began to spin and tilt on its axis. She attempted to raise her arms up in the traditional gymnastics salute, but stumbled instead.

"Whoa!" Colton was at her side in an instant. "Are you all right?"

She nodded, although it wasn't true. She vaguely remembered Colton saying "Thank you" into the microphone before he stopped the music and led her back to their table.

"Are you dizzy? Because that's a sign of a concussion, Nat."

Natalie nodded. "I know. I was a little dizzy after I fell earlier, but I thought it was nothing."

"Natalie!" he scolded. "You were supposed to tell me."

"It probably wasn't smart to flip around after the accident this morning."

Colton sat down on the chair next to hers. "Was that just this morning?" He shook his head. "Seems like days ago."

"I know," she agreed.

He put one arm around her and took hold of her forearm with the other. "Should we go to the hospital?" he asked with such concern in his voice.

"No. It's fine. I'll take it easy from now on."

"Are you sure? I don't like this."

She saw the worry in his eyes. "I promise to tell you if I feel even the slightest bit off again, OK?"

He squeezed her arm. "OK."

A woman took the stage then and began belting out an off-key version of "I Will Always Love You" by Whitney Houston.

"I think that's our cue." Colton placed some cash on the table to cover their bill. "Are you good to go?"

Natalie nodded and stood slowly, only slight dizziness remaining. "I'm good."

He kept one arm around her back and one on her arm as they walked toward the exit. She never thought she could be so happy to have a concussion.

11
For the Night

When Natalie emerged from the restaurant after using the restroom, she found Colton leaning against the passenger side of his car, scrolling through something on his phone.

He looked up as she approached. "You probably shouldn't drive."

"Probably not."

He opened the door for her.

"Or sleep," she said. "I think I'm supposed to stay awake if I have a concussion."

"That's a myth. You actually should get rest so you can heal. I just have to wake you every couple hours and make sure you're able to talk to me."

She climbed in, tugged the seatbelt across her chest, and gazed up into Colton's eyes. "If I don't wake up ..." The belt clicked as it locked into place as if she had planned it for dramatic effect.

Colton's shoulders sank. "Please don't go into a coma on me."

She smiled up at him. "I'll do my best."

He closed her door and moved around to the driver's side, holding out his phone as he climbed in. "Hey, I found a place for us to sleep tonight."

Natalie's forehead creased. "I thought we were driving straight through the night."

"It's been a long day. I'm tired, and you can't drive."

The idea of staying in a hotel with him freaked her out. "Maybe we could stop at a rest stop for an hour or two and sleep in the car."

"That's ridiculous. We're not sleeping in the car."

"I don't know if I'm comfortable staying at a hotel with you," she said. "I'll need my own room."

"Not a hotel." He handed her the phone and started the car. "It seems every town along this highway has some kind of festival going on this weekend. Every place that wasn't a fleabag motel was all booked up."

She read what was on the screen. "What's Mountain Ridge Resort?"

Colton pulled out onto the road. "It's a campground an hour from here."

"Why pay to sleep in the car at a campground when we can sleep in the car at a rest area?"

"I have a tent."

"You have a tent?" Her eyebrows raised. "*With* you?"

"In my trunk." He pointed his thumb over his shoulder toward the back of the car.

"Don't you think the car will be more comfortable than the hard ground?"

"I have an air mattress." He glanced her way. "And a two-person sleeping bag."

Her eyes narrowed, and her mouth shifted to the side and scrunched up in disapproval. "No way. Not happening."

"You can have the sleeping bag," he told her.

"So, you just carry camping gear with you wherever you go?"

"We camped out at Grant's a couple weeks ago."

Natalie needed no more explanation than that. Everyone knew about parties at Grant's house, where people would crash for entire weekends. She didn't want to think about who he meant when he said *we*. Because it was very likely that he and Lexi had slept in that tent together, and if she let her mind wander, well ... she didn't have to be a genius to know what they had probably done in the cozy two-person sleeping bag.

A jealousy that she hadn't expected reared its ugly head. Colton didn't belong to her in any way, but she grew more and more upset the more she thought about it.

"You're quiet," Colton broke through her bitter thoughts. "You OK with camping?"

"Fine." Her mind played out several scenarios, from her sleeping in the car by herself to her snuggled up in Colton's arms. The latter made her stomach flip.

Colton drove on, following the navigation system along some

Pennsylvania roads until they reached the campground. He stopped at the registration office and checked them in. All the while, Natalie's anxiety ramped up at the idea of sleeping in the same space as Colton.

He returned to the car and drove through the campground toward their site. Up ahead, a small group of people were gathered around a camper with a sign that said "Hosts: Wilmot and Elinore Beezley."

As they drove past, the sound of banjo and harmonica music floated in through their windows.

Colton started bouncing his knee and tapping it jokingly, which broke through her nerves and made her laugh.

He stopped at the end of the drive next to a tent campsite on a hill overlooking the forested valley below.

Natalie walked over to the edge of their site and gazed out at the beauty. The sun hung low in the western sky, almost touching the mountaintops. "Nice view."

"I'll say."

She glanced back over her shoulder and found him watching her, and a blush creeped over her cheeks. *Gosh, he's good with the pickup lines.*

Natalie would never admit it to Colton, but she was happy to be there. After eleven hours on the road, she was ready to get out of his car for a while. Sitting in a vehicle for hours on end wasn't doing anything to improve her stiff neck.

Colton popped the trunk and pulled out the tent bag and a flashlight. "We need to get this set up before it gets too dark." He dumped the contents onto the ground and unrolled the tent in the center of their grassy campsite.

"What can I do?" she asked.

"Grab those poles and get them laid out."

Natalie straightened out the tent poles and placed them on the ground. By the time she had finished, Colton had the green dome tent laid out and ready to assemble. Once they had it set up, Colton went around and staked it down while Natalie opened up the rain fly and threw it as best she could over the top of the tent.

"Like this?" she asked as it slipped further down one side.

"Only if you want to get wet if it rains."

"Hey, it's not easy."

He chuckled as he adjusted the rain fly to the proper position.

They worked together to get it attached to the top of the tent and staked to the ground.

"Voila!" Colton proclaimed when it was all set up. "We make a good team."

She liked that he said that.

Colton left Natalie admiring their handiwork and retrieved the air mattress, pump, and sleeping bag from his trunk.

She watched as he unzipped the door to the tent and disappeared inside. Nervous butterflies zigzagged around in her stomach at the humming of the air pump. The air pump that was inflating the mattress. The mattress they would be sleeping on. Together.

The sun disappeared behind the hilltops, leaving the sky beautiful shades of pink and purple. Birds were chirping in a nearby tree, and a rabbit was hopping down the side of the hill. The banjo music was faint, but still going on.

"We should go listen to the music before they stop for the night," Natalie called out to Colton.

"Huh?" he replied.

She walked over to the tent door and found Colton without a shirt—again—working on the air mattress. "I said we should go listen to the music before they stop playing."

Colton wiped the sweat from his brow with his wadded-up shirt.

"If ... if you keep dirtying all your shirts, you're going to run out of clothes before we even get to the beach."

"It's hot in here," he explained.

Natalie stepped in and was surprised at the difference in temperature, especially since they had only just set it up. She moved to the side and unzipped the window. "We need to let some air in." She did the same on the other side as Colton stopped the pump and pushed the valve in to trap the air.

He lay back on the mattress and bounced a little. "Lay down and see if this is firm enough for you." He patted the spot beside him.

"Uh ... I'll take your word for it."

He raised an eyebrow at her. "Don't you trust me?"

Were her palms sweating? She rubbed them on her jeans and quickly exited the tent, needing distance. The air was probably ten degrees cooler outside, and her cheeks were once again on fire thinking about the sleeping arrangements. She walked to the car so she could keep moving and retrieved her water bottle, swigging down the last of it. She noticed Colton's and grabbed it for him.

He was emerging from the tent when she approached.

"Thanks." He took the bottle from her outstretched hand and proceeded to down it in one long steady chug. He started to put his sweaty shirt back on, then stopped with his head poked through the hole, one arm in, one arm out. He tilted his head like he was listening for something. "I don't hear the music anymore."

"Maybe they're done for the night." She pouted.

It suddenly picked up again.

"Aw, yeah." He yanked his shirt the rest of the way on and started walking down the lane toward the hosts. "You comin'?"

Natalie grinned and jogged to catch up to him.

When they reached the hosts' campsite, they stood to the rear of a group who had settled in with their lawn chairs for a listen. A few campers standing nearby welcomed them. One older man even offered Natalie his seat, but she declined.

Colton elbowed Natalie.

She saw him patting his hand on the side of his thigh, bouncing his knee like he had when they drove in. She elbowed him back and tried to keep from laughing.

Then he started tapping the back of his hand against her outer thigh to the same rhythm he had before.

She raised an eyebrow at him, but he ignored her and bobbed his head to the music.

The Beezleys looked like their name, if that made any sense at all. Wilmot wore denim bib overalls and a red and blue plaid shirt. He had silver hair and a bushy silver beard. Elinore had wavy grey hair twisted in a tight bun at the nape of her neck. She wore a rainbow tie-dyed t-shirt, yellow cotton shorts, and white ankle socks with brown sandals. One thing they had in common was a mouthful of crooked teeth when they smiled.

Wilmot's fingers moved over the banjo strings, while Elinore played the harmonica expertly. They performed three songs in a row and had the audience clapping. Even Natalie and Colton clapped along.

Natalie loved every moment. A banjo and harmonica duet wasn't an everyday occurrence. This trip kept getting more and more interesting. She wondered if Colton thought the same.

When the mini concert had concluded, twilight had settled over the campground. A few of the campers hung around to talk with the hosts, while others headed back to their campsites.

Colton wandered over to the Beezleys. "That was a lot of fun. Thanks."

"Oh, you're welcome." Wilmot shook his hand.

"Where're you two from?" Elinore asked.

"Michigan," he replied. "We're on our way to Virginia Beach."

"How long you here?" Wilmot set his banjo on the table by their camper.

"We're back on the road in the morning."

"Just for tonight then?" he asked.

The two of them nodded in reply.

"Well, we're so happy to have you."

"Thank you," Natalie said.

"Oh, there's a chance of thunderstorms tonight," Elinore added.

Natalie looked southwest toward the approaching clouds, and her stomach dropped.

"If you need anything at all, including a dry place to hide out, please don't hesitate to come by. Our door is always open."

"Thanks," Colton replied. "I waterproofed the tent, so we should be good."

Wilmot and Elinore wished them goodnight, and they walked back toward their campsite.

Colton elbowed Natalie's arm. "What's up? You look like someone ate all your chicken parm."

"I can't handle storms," she mumbled.

"We'll be all right. If we have to, we'll jump in the car and wait it out."

She didn't reply. Every bad thing that had ever happened in her life had happened during a thunderstorm. Storms only ever brought unhappiness her way.

Colton must've sensed how serious she was. "Don't worry. I'll be with you the whole time." He put his arm around her and gave her a squeeze.

It did little to calm her nerves.

12
Camping

Natalie grabbed her bags from the trunk and lugged them into the darkening tent with her. She unzipped her suitcase and turned on the flashlight to find the pj's she had packed for the week. She dropped them onto the air mattress and pointed the light at them, wondering if maybe she should sleep in her jeans and a sweatshirt rather than the spaghetti strap tank top and cotton pajama shorts. But it was still warm in the tent and she could climb inside the sleeping bag before Colton ever had a chance to see her, so she opted for the pj's.

With the flashlight turned off, there was still the faintest light within the tent. She crossed her arms over her stomach and grabbed the bottom edge of her shirt, tugging it up over her head just as she heard the zip of the tent door. Her shirt came up over her face in time to see Colton staring at her chest, covered only in a lacy white bra. She yanked her shirt down, covering herself as fast as humanly possible.

"Don't look!" she cried. "Get out!"

He averted his eyes. "Sorry."

But she caught that cute little smirk as he swiftly turned around, closing the tent door on his way out.

"I told you I was changing," she called after him.

"No, you didn't."

Wait, he was right. She hadn't said the words. She had taken her suitcase to the tent with her, assuming he would know, and then he had wandered off to the bathroom. "Well, I'm changing."

"I barely saw anything. It's dark in there."

"Right." She knew he was lying. If there was enough light for her to see his face, there was enough for him to get an eyeful.

"I'm sorry," he said.

"Knock next time." Flustered, she whipped her shirt off, tugged her jeans down as quickly as possible, caught her foot in one of the legs, and tumbled onto the air mattress. She lay there in the near dark, staring up at the top of the tent, her jeans stuck on her leg, wearing nothing but her bra and underwear. Something about the moment and the entire situation struck her as funny, and she began to laugh.

"What's so funny?" Colton asked through the wall of the tent.

She couldn't answer through her laughter.

"Knock knock." Colton started unzipping the tent door again.

"No!" she cried, trying to control her laughter. "Not yet."

"Girls are so slow. I would've stripped down in two seconds flat."

This only made Natalie laugh harder, until she heard a subtle rumble in the distance. "Was that thunder?"

"Yes, so hurry up before I get stuck out here in the rain."

She yanked her foot from the jeans, threw on her pajamas, jumped up, and unzipped the tent door, hauling Colton in by his arm.

"That's what I'm talkin' about." He chuckled.

She didn't care what he meant by that. All she cared about was having him close as another distant rumble sounded, causing a chill to run through her body.

"I need to change too, ya know." He pointed at the door.

"No way. I'm not going out there right now." She crossed her arms over her chest and sat down on the mattress.

Colton turned on the flashlight, and his expression changed when he saw her face. "Why are you so scared?"

Natalie swallowed hard, but didn't respond.

"It's only a little thunder," he said.

She shook her head. Or was it her body shaking? She wasn't sure.

He sat down next to her and put an arm around her lower back. "Do you want to sit in the car?"

"I can't," she managed. She couldn't move. It was always the same. One rumble of thunder and she was frozen in place.

"You're trembling." He scooted closer, tightening his arm around her.

She turned into him and wrapped her arms around his waist, burying her head in his shoulder.

"Hey, it's all right." He squeezed her tight and held her until the trembling began to subside.

Natalie let go and saw what she thought was honest-to-goodness concern in his eyes.

"Are you tired?" he asked.

She nodded. "I'm beat."

"You can use the sleeping bag. I'll just sleep on top."

"I'm kind of warm right now." She lay back on top of the sleeping bag and closed her eyes.

"I'll set the alarm on my phone so I can check on you in a couple hours."

"Good idea." She said it knowing she probably wouldn't be able to sleep during the storm anyway.

She heard the rustling of Colton moving around and peeked to see what he was doing just as his jeans dropped to the ground, leaving him in only green plaid boxer shorts. She snapped her eyelids shut so he wouldn't catch her watching him. The air mattress lifted as he sat down on the edge then lay back next to her. The tent went dark as he clicked off the flashlight.

The pitter patter of raindrops hitting the top of the tent began, followed by the sounds of a steadier rain as the storm neared.

"What if we get struck by lightning?" Her eyes searched for him but found only darkness.

"We won't get struck by lightning."

"But we're in a tiny tent on top of a mountain. We're just asking for it." She couldn't stop herself from shaking again. Lightning flashed, and she saw his face for a brief moment.

"Come here." His hand was suddenly on her hip, tugging her closer.

And then she was where she had dreamed of being so many times—in Colton's arms. His right arm was draped over her hip and around her back.

"I've got you," he whispered.

Lightning struck close by, thunder boomed, and Natalie screamed.

Colton started to laugh.

"Don't laugh," she whimpered.

"I'm sorry." He did it again.

"Stop." She smacked his chest.

But he couldn't stop, which made her laugh too.

"You're adorable." He began to run his hand up and down her back comfortingly.

A chill ran through her, but she didn't have time to think about her reaction to him, because lightning lit up the tent followed by a loud crack.

She stifled another scream. "Talk to me," she blurted.

"About what?" Colton asked.

"I don't care. Anything. Distract me," Natalie pleaded.

"I can think of lots of ways to distract you," he chuckled.

She smacked his chest again, harder this time.

"*Ow!*"

The rain began pouring down hard outside. Tears burned in her eyes, threatening to fall. A sudden loud boom made her jump. She could almost feel the sting of her cheek where her mother had slapped her once just for breaking a glass. With each flash, her mind's eye saw the devastation on her father's face when he found Mom lying on the floor of the kitchen with an empty pill bottle in her hand. Every crack of thunder replayed the slam of the door the night Mom walked out on them.

Lightning flashed again, revealing the look on her face.

"You're really afraid, aren't you?" he asked.

"I told you, I can't handle storms."

He rubbed her back some more. "I sing."

"What?"

"My talent. I can sing."

"You can?" Her voice trembled. "I've never heard you sing in one talent show at school."

"That's because school talent shows are lame."

"No, they're not. There's some real talent in our school. Those guys who played original songs their band wrote are really good. Somebody said they signed with an agent."

"That's true," he replied. "I've never sung in public before or anything, mostly in the shower."

"What songs? And please don't say rap."

He laughed. "Of course, rap." He started reciting lyrics from one of the songs that had played earlier that day.

"No! That's not singing." She covered her ears with her hands.

"What? Yes, it is."

"Tell me you sing something with an actual melody."

Thunder rumbled again, and he tightened his arm around her. "Elvis."

"Elvis Presley?"

"My grandpa loved Elvis. He died when I was ten, and I got all his records and his record player."

"Very vintage."

"Very."

"Your dad's dad or your mom's dad?" she asked.

"Mom's. He was the best. I remember fishing with him off this little dock behind his house. Even though I caught the tiniest fish, he always made such a huge deal of it, like it was some record-size bass or something."

The tent lit up as the sky flashed, and she saw his sentimental smile. Every time he revealed something new about himself, she felt closer to him. And this memory of his grandpa was absolutely endearing.

"What's your favorite Elvis song?" she asked.

He cleared his throat and began to sing the first few lines of "I Can't Help Falling in Love With You." His voice was low and smooth, soothing her worries, calming her trembles away.

"*Mmmm.* I love that song." She closed her eyes and listened.

As he finished the chorus, she peeked at him from under heavy eyelids. "You really *can* sing," she mumbled, half asleep.

He continued on, but Natalie didn't hear the end of the song or any more of the storm. Colton's voice had lulled her to sleep.

A crack of thunder woke Natalie from a dead sleep. She jumped, and Colton did too. His arm was still wrapped around her, only he had moved closer so they were snuggled up against each other.

He rolled over and tapped the home button on his phone, illuminating the tent temporarily.

"What time is it?" Natalie asked.

"Two-thirty. You OK?"

She nodded, but something felt off. Something felt … wet. She reached back and touched the mattress behind her. "Oh no!" She sat up as the tent faded to dark again.

"What?" He tapped his phone to give them more light.

"The tent leaked." Natalie crawled to the end of the air mattress to escape the wet spot.

Colton sat up and turned on the flashlight. He leaned over to feel the sleeping bag and directed the light on the mattress then upward to find the leak. The wind whipped the tent walls and rain was blowing under the the rain fly and dripping in through the open window.

"*Someone* forgot to close the windows," he teased.

She laid a hand over her heart. "This is *my* fault?"

"I mean, if you had closed them, your side of the bed would be dry. I guess we'll both have to sleep on my side so you won't get dripped on." He winked at her.

"I'll take my chances."

Colton chuckled as he stood and zipped both of the windows shut, pointing the flashlight at the puddle on the opposite side of the tent floor. He rifled around in his bag and tossed a towel at Natalie, covering her head.

She peeked out from beneath it and watched as he moved their bags away from the puddle. "Are the bags wet?"

"Mine's a little damp, but it'll dry. Could you stand up for a second?"

She did as he asked, crossing her arms over her chest at a sudden chill. He slid the entire mattress toward the middle of the tent, away from the leaky window. Taking the towel from Natalie, he wiped at the damp edge of the sleeping bag before placing it over the wet spot and lying down on that side of the mattress. "You can have the dry side."

"Oh, thanks." She lay down and faced away from him as the flashlight turned off.

"Can you hand me my phone?"

She reached for his phone and handed it over to him. The tent lit up again as he turned it on.

"I'm glad the storm woke you," he said.

"Why?" She looked back at him.

"I'm supposed to be checking to make sure you don't go into a coma from your concussion. My alarm didn't go off for some reason."

"Oh."

Colton leaned over her and held his phone close to her face, staring deep into her eyes.

"What're you doing?"

"I'm checking to see if your pupils are dilated."

Natalie pushed against his chest.

"Can you tell me your name?"

Natalie giggled at that.

"I'm serious."

"My name's Deb," she replied.

Confusion crossed his face.

"Are you my friend Davey?" She grinned.

Colton chuckled and clicked his phone off. "You're obviously not in a coma."

"Maybe *you* are, and this is all a dream," she teased.

His hand came to rest on her hip once more. "Not a bad dream."

She smiled to herself before removing his hand.

"Why are you so afraid of storms?" he asked.

Natalie was silent for several beats. "Just bad memories."

"Like what?"

"Stuff to do with my mom."

He laid his hand on her arm.

"Bad stuff always seems to happen during storms. When the weather gets severe like this, all those moments surface, and it takes me back to things I would rather not remember."

"I'm sorry."

"It's not your fault." The cool air seeping into the tent made her shiver.

"Are you cold?"

She nodded even though he couldn't see her. "The temperature must've dropped."

"Yeah, it's a little chilly. You can have the sleeping bag, Natalie."

She unzipped the edge of the sleeping bag and snuggled down deep. The warmth from their bodies lying on top had heated the inside, making it nice and cozy.

Colton shifted atop the sleeping bag, and she felt bad, leaving him in the cold.

"We can share it," she told him.

"You sure?"

"I'm sure." Was she, really? The idea of him next to her in the sleeping bag released the butterflies again. "But no funny business."

He chuckled as he climbed in next to her, then groaned. "It's a little wet over here."

"You're only saying that to get on my side."

He moved closer and rolled to face her, still respecting her space. But the next flash of lightning and clap of thunder had Natalie scooting toward him.

"Hey, tell me what the poem said."

"Huh?"

"The poem I wrote you when we were kids," he replied.

"I don't remember," she mumbled.

"I know you do. Come on. Tell me."

Thunder boomed, and she forced her brain to remember the lines of the poem. "Fine. It said 'There once was a girl named Natalie. She climbed up the jungle gym with me. She likes candy bars and stickers. Her hair is brown like Snickers. One day, she's going to marry me.'"

Colton rolled onto his back and cracked up laughing.

"See, I told you it was good for a six-year old." A sudden gust of wind and a loud crack that might have been a branch breaking startled her.

"I was a real charmer, wasn't I?" He brought his arm around her again and rubbed her back comfortingly as he had before. But this time, his fingers met the skin of her lower back, where her shirt had hitched up, and he froze.

"You still are," she replied softly.

"Maybe you can make some good memories to replace the bad." The way he whispered into her ear felt very intimate.

Natalie didn't move at first and neither did Colton.

But with the next rumble of thunder, she moved an inch closer and wrapped her arm around him, resting her hand on his lower back.

Colton began to softly caress her skin with his thumb, still not making any sudden moves.

A struggle took place in Natalie's mind between her longing to trace her fingers over Colton's back and her fear of what might happen if she did. Against her better judgment, she moved her hand and he seemed to take that as an invitation. His hand slid under the edge of her shirt, traveling over the bare skin of her back, leaving goosebumps in the wake of his feathery touch.

She held her breath as unfamiliar sensations flowed over her body. His lips touched her forehead then, his breathing shallow. Her breaths were in sync with his, and he moved closer still.

Warning bells began to sound in her brain. She had always been adamant that she would not sleep with a guy before marriage, and the thought of cheating or being the one someone cheated with was appalling to her. Especially after her mom's history. But in this moment, with Colton's lips so close to touching hers, she was tempted to give in. Her heart was beating so fast in her chest that she thought it might burst.

Lightning illuminated the tent. Their eyes met, then darkness enclosed them again. She could feel the warmth of his breath against her face as the wind whistled outside.

She had to stop this before it went too far, before she couldn't anymore. But the blood pumping rapidly through her veins was making it impossible for her to find her words.

God, please help me.

Another flash and she saw the intensity in his eyes just before his eyelids slipped shut. Darkness again as his lips brushed against hers, soft as a whisper.

"Wait." Natalie said as the tent lit up again, flickering like a strobe light.

He leaned away. "What is it?"

"You have a girlfriend." The words popped out of her mouth, and she silently thanked God for helping her to speak.

He said nothing for a few beats, then rolled onto his back and let out a breath. "I know."

"A girlfriend who will make my life a living hell if she finds out about this."

"I know." The flashlight clicked on, and he rolled on his side to face her. His expression was pensive, and he remained quiet at first, seemingly deep in thought. "Six months ago, I never would've thought twice about this. But now ..." He reached over and moved a hair that had fallen over her eye. "I've never been so afraid to mess things up with someone before. I've never cared so much about doing the right thing. Until you."

Natalie's brow furrowed. "Are these lines? Is this what you say to all the other girls?"

He frowned, looking insulted. "I don't usually talk much to girls I ... *camp* with."

"Oh my gosh." Repulsed, Natalie pushed him away and jumped up to standing, staring down at the sleeping bag draped open to reveal Colton's bare chest. "I don't even want to know how many girls you've hooked up with in there." She shivered at the thought.

Colton sat up and looked at her. "I'm not gonna lie. There have been a few."

"*Ewww*. Disgusting. I cannot stay here with you. I can't believe I climbed in there in the first place." Natalie was just as disgusted with herself for almost letting something happen with him.

"It's not about hooking up right now. It's different with you."

"This was such a huge mistake." She turned her back to him.

"Natalie, you aren't listening to me."

"I heard you." She crossed her arms over her chest.

"Did you?"

She nodded. "You're saying you care."

"Yes."

"About me."

"Yeah." He stood up then and stepped closer, turning her around to look at him. "You're sweet and good and ... boring, but in an interesting, I-want-to-figure-you-out kind of way."

She looked away, but he touched her chin to get her to look at him again.

"I like you, Natalie."

Was she hearing things? Did he actually admit to liking her? A tingling sensation remained even after his fingertips left her chin.

"There's something about you that makes me want to tell you everything about myself, about my life, and I want to know everything there is to know about you too."

She stared at him, dumbfounded.

"Aren't you going to say anything?" he asked.

"Is this a prank? Something you and Lexi cooked up for me?"

She might as well have slapped him across the face. "Are you serious right now?"

She wasn't serious. Not really. She believed he *was* being genuine with her, but it was all she could think to say to steer the conversation from its current course, to keep him at arm's length, especially after what almost happened between them.

"I'm standing here telling you how much I care about you. I've told you things I've never told another soul. And still you think I could possibly be messing with you?" Exasperated, he climbed back into the sleeping bag and rolled so his back was facing her.

"I'm sorry, but none of this trip has been normal, especially the fact that I'm taking it with *you*."

He peeked back over his shoulder at her as she sat down on the tent floor next to the mattress.

"Honesty time, OK?"

He rolled to face her again and propped his head up on his arm.

"I've had a crush on you since that day in elementary school."

The right corner of his mouth curved up a little.

"You were so cute and so sweet, and even as the years went by and we all grew up and changed, I always held this special place in my heart for you. Even when I saw you acting all rude and cocky and dating every horrible, self-involved, loose girl in the school, part of me hoped I was wrong about you, that deep down you were still that sweet kid who was my first boyfriend."

He cocked his head. "I'm still that kid," he assured her.

"I mean, I've seen glimpses of him today, but am I really enough to bring you back from all the places you've been, all the partying and drinking, all your trophies—sports and otherwise?" She cleared her throat. "I mean ... I'm boring. You said so yourself."

"I like your brand of boring." His adorable smile brought out the dimple in his right cheek.

"We're just very different people. You're popular. I'm *so* not. You've got money, and my family barely scrapes by. You're ... experienced." She pointed to herself. "Me, not so much."

He smirked.

"And I don't plan to be. So if that's what you're thinking, then you've got another thing coming."

"It's not," he replied.

She wanted to believe him.

"Just so you know, I haven't had a girl in here in a long time."

"Define long time."

He thought for a second. "A year."

Natalie wrinkled her nose. She didn't care how long it had been. She didn't want to think about other girls being in the tent at all.

He looked up into her eyes. "I can't take back the things I've done in the past. No matter how much I wish I could."

"I know." Did he really wish that?

"And I can't help it if I'm attracted to you. Opposites attract, or so I've heard." That smile of his was enough to ruin her for every other guy.

"What're we really talking about here, Colton? I mean, yes, I like you. Of course, I do. But what does that even mean?"

"A lot." He sat up. "It could change things."

"What things?"

He gave no answer.

"Once we get to Virginia Beach, you're going to meet up with Grant and Lexi and your friends, and things will go back to the way they were before. You'll go back to not knowing me again."

"That's not what I want."

"But that's what will happen. That's what always happens in situations like this."

"Everything's different now." He crawled closer to sit on his knees in front of her. "Don't you feel it?"

"It's just the excitement of taking this trip together. It's all thrilling right now, getting to know someone new, but we're both off to college in the fall. Far away from each other."

"How far?"

"I'm going to Arizona on a gymnastics scholarship," she answered.

His eyes widened. "That *is* far."

"And I'm not looking to get attached to someone and then have to walk away in three months."

His eyes narrowed. "You're very logical, aren't you?"

"Did you expect anything else?"

"Not really." A smile crossed his face just before his hand came to rest on hers. "I don't want to not know you."

She nodded once in agreement. "Maybe we'll stay friends." She hoped it would be true, but doubted it.

He touched her cheek, his thumb brushing against her bottom lip. "Friends who make out?"

She pushed against his chest and sent him tumbling back onto the sleeping bag, laughing and holding his chest as if he'd been wounded. She rolled her eyes and reached for her bag, grabbing a sweatshirt before she lay down on top of the sleeping bag instead of climbing back in next to Colton. It was better this way, and the idea of lying where Colton had been with other girls made her a little sick to her stomach.

"Why six months ago?" she asked as her mind played over everything.

"Huh?"

"You said six months ago, you never would've thought twice about ... this. What changed in six months?"

"Nothing."

She didn't believe him, but she didn't push. The storms had begun to pass, but she could no longer sleep. And she realized he had gotten her through it. She had been so focused on him and their conversations and what was happening between them that she almost forgot about the frightful weather outside. And she had been too distracted to let her mind dwell on the past.

13
Sermon on the Mount

The sound of birds chirping in a nearby tree woke her. She lay still for a while, listening, eyes closed, enjoying the feeling of fingers slipping through her hair over and over. Her eyes flew open when she realized they were Colton's fingers, and she was greeted with a nice view of his solid bare chest. She had snuggled up next to him at some point in the night and now lay in his arms, his upper body sticking out of the sleeping bag, her head resting on his chest.

More than anything, she wanted to stay put. She wanted to forget the fact that there was a Lexi and kiss him and touch him and do whatever he wanted to do with her this morning. But she couldn't. She knew she couldn't. It would be a moment, a one-time thing, and she wanted more than that, she deserved more than that.

She wiggled in his arms, and he let out a low groan that nearly made her give in and kiss him.

"Morning." He squeezed his arms tighter around her.

"Morning," she responded quietly.

He unwound his arms from her and sat up.

She watched him, all naked from the waist up. He really was a beautiful guy, especially with that messy bed head he was sporting at the moment. A giggle escaped her before she could stop it.

He looked back at her. "What?"

"Nothing." She glanced up at his hair.

He attempted to smooth it down, then turned to her again. "Hey, I'm not the only one with crazy morning hair."

She sat up and gathered her hair into a messy bun on top of her head, securing it with one of the hair ties she always kept around her wrist for gymnastics.

"Oh my gosh." He stared at her.

"What?"

"I didn't think you could possibly get any cuter." He gazed up at her messy bun. "I was so wrong."

She blushed. It was nice to be admired, to feel beautiful, especially in Colton's eyes. But she had to keep reminding herself that once they reached their destination, this would be over.

"How are you feeling?" Colton asked. "Does your neck still hurt?"

She shifted her head from side to side. "Still stiff, but better, I think."

"Good." He reached for her knee.

She jerked it away from his hand.

"I wanted to see how your wound is healing."

"My *wound*? It was a scratch. Yours was a wound." She waved her finger in a circular motion to get him to turn around.

He rolled his eyes and turned.

She leaned forward and gently touched the bandaged area on his back. It appeared less red and had started scabbing over. She couldn't help but notice the goosebumps that had spread over his skin at her touch.

"How's it look, Doc?" His voice wavered a little.

"You'll survive." She patted his back and moved away.

Colton stood and grabbed a t-shirt from his bag, pulling it over his head. "Do you mind if I go for a quick run?"

"Go ahead."

"Do you want to come along?"

"Nah. I'll get cleaned up and get my stuff packed."

He unzipped the door to the tent and zipped her in. "I'll be back."

"OK." She sank down onto the air mattress again, her mind replaying every minute of last night and this morning. She shook it off and gathered her things, heading off to the shower facilities and away from the tent.

The campground was filled with the aroma of campers' breakfasts, some being prepared over the open fire.

"That smells so good," Colton said as they finished taking down the tent and began rolling it up.

"My stomach just growled," Natalie said.

"Yeah, I heard it." He laughed.

She scrunched up her nose at him.

Just then, Wilmot and Elinore arrived at their site.

"Good morning, you two," Elinore greeted them. "We thought you might like some breakfast." She opened the bag she'd been carrying and revealed two plastic containers with lids.

"That's so sweet of you," Natalie said as she took one.

Colton dropped the half-rolled tent and took the container Elinore handed him, popping open the lid to reveal sausage, bacon, scrambled eggs, and a blueberry muffin. He stepped to Elinore and hugged her firmly. "Thank you."

She chuckled. "You're more than welcome."

"We thought you might like to join us for a little Sunday morning service at the gazebo." Wilmot motioned toward the other end of the campground.

"Oh, that sounds nice, but we're packing up to get back on the road," Natalie explained.

"We can go if you want," Colton said through a bite of muffin. "We've got time."

She was surprised by his response. He didn't seem like the kind of guy that went to church or was interested in anything remotely spiritual.

"Well, great," Wilmot replied with his crooked-toothed smile. "It's getting started now, so come on over if you want. You can bring your breakfast with you."

The sweet couple walked away, and Natalie looked over at Colton. "You really want to go to church?"

He chomped on a piece of bacon. "Sure, why not."

"I didn't think you were much of a church-goer."

"You would be correct." Colton started walking.

A small group of campers were seated in the yard around the gazebo. On the steps were a man playing guitar and a woman leading the group in song. Colton and Natalie took a couple empty seats at the back, and a woman approached and handed them a paper with song lyrics on it. Natalie immediately joined in singing the next hymn, one she already knew well from her own church. Colton used the song sheet and sang along.

"What a friend we have in Jesus, all our sins and griefs to bear," they sang. "What a privilege to carry everything to God in prayer."

Colton elbowed her, and she found him grinning at her.

She stopped singing. "What?"

"Look who has another talent."

She shook her head and continued. "Oh, what peace we often forfeit, oh, what needless pain we bear, all because we do not carry everything to God in prayer."

They sounded good together, singing in perfect harmony, and she wondered why he had never joined choir at school.

"Can we find a friend so faithful, who will all our sorrows share? Jesus knows our every weakness. Take it to the Lord in prayer."

Colton quieted as everyone else sang. He seemed affected.

"What's wrong?" Natalie asked.

"Nothing." He blew it off.

The song came to an end, and they sat and listened to Wilmot speak from the Sermon on the Mount in the book of Matthew, which seemed fitting with them being on top of a mountain and all. He focused on the passages about not worrying about your life.

"Behold the fowls of the air: for they sow not, neither do they reap, nor gather into barns; yet your heavenly Father feedeth them. Are ye not much better than they?"

It had been a long time since she heard someone quote the King James Version of the Bible. Her Dad often read her verses from that version. He said it sounded better to him than the newer translations.

Wilmot's words seemed to cause Colton to fidget in his seat.

"But seek ye first the kingdom of God and his righteousness; and all these things shall be added unto you. Take therefore no thought for the morrow: for the morrow shall take thought for the things of itself."

Colton glanced at his phone and leaned closer. "We should go soon," he whispered.

"OK." She took his lead, and they left discretely.

Wilmot spotted them, but continued speaking and gave them a friendly wave goodbye.

"Is everything OK?" she asked as they walked back to the campsite.

"Yeah, why?"

"You seemed bothered or something back there."

He gazed over at her. "What if our accident was no accident?"

She looked at him curiously. "What do you mean?"

"I mean, like, what if it was meant to happen?"

Natalie laughed. "Like, you were meant to drive like a crazy person, and I was meant to crash into that other guy's car?"

He let out a little chuckle. "I guess that sounds kind of stupid, huh?"

"I didn't say that." She regretted her thoughtless reaction.

"Never mind." He waved a hand at her.

"I'm sorry for laughing. It's not stupid, Colton. Tell me what you're thinking."

"It's nothing. I was just thinking out loud." He shook his head as if returning to his senses.

"Colton."

"So ... you're a church girl."

She sighed at the change of subject, knowing he wasn't going to tell her. "I go to church, yeah."

"That explains it."

"Explains what?"

"Why you're so boring." He winked at her.

"Going to church doesn't make me boring."

He grinned at her. "I told you, I like your kind of boring."

She smirked. "Whatever."

"I'm saying, church suits you. It's a compliment."

"Well, I can never tell with you."

"You will," he said.

"I will what?"

"You'll figure out my sense of humor."

They walked on in silence. She wanted to remind him that she wouldn't figure him out, that they would go back to not knowing each other in a matter of hours. But she let it be, and they went back to work packing up the tent and loading their things into his trunk.

When Colton ran off to the restroom, Natalie stood in the center of their campsite, staring at the rounded, forest-covered mountaintops before her. A moment of peace was exactly what she needed. A moment away from Colton and her growing attraction to him. A moment to clear her head.

She closed her eyes and opened her heart in a prayer. God already knew what she was feeling, what she needed, without a word being said. She felt him close as she remembered Wilmot's message. *Seek ye first the kingdom of God.* Those words were as familiar to her as her own name. She had heard them since she was a little girl, sang them in a chorus at church, read them every day as she passed by the frame that hung in the entryway of their house. It was like her mantra, so the fact that Wilmot spoke those very words felt simply providential.

Colton's words about their accident hung in her thoughts as well. She wished he would've let her in and explained what he meant. What was he thinking? Something had obviously sparked his question—something prompted by the song or the verses Wilmot quoted.

"What ya thinkin' about?"

Colton's voice made her jump.

"Sorry, you looked deep in thought."

"Soaking in the silence before I have to get back in that ugly yellow beast and listen to rap the rest of the way."

His chin dropped. "Ugly? Are you kidding? My baby is beautiful."

"Why yellow, though? You could've gone with red or black."

"Yellow looks sharp with the black stripes."

"If you say so." She rolled her eyes.

"It does."

"And you want people to see you coming a mile away."

"What's wrong with that?"

She shrugged. "Attention hog."

"Little miss boring."

"*Ooh*, good one." She rolled her eyes again.

"Hey, if you don't like my car, you don't have to ride in it."

She narrowed her eyes at him and stuck out her tongue.

He chuckled. "That's mature."

They climbed into the car and drove slowly through the campground. It appeared the church service had just let out as the campers scattered.

Elinore saw them coming and walked toward their car.

Natalie rolled down her window.

She leaned down to see both of them. "So glad you stayed with us. Hope you have a safe trip to Virginia."

"Thanks. It's lovely here. Maybe we'll come back one day," Natalie replied. She said the words before she really thought about them, and glanced over at Colton, who was already smirking at her.

He smiled in that adorable way that made his dimple show. "Yeah, maybe we will."

14
Used

How much longer to Virginia Beach?" Natalie asked when they were finally back on the road.

Colton tapped the screen on the GPS. "Looks like about seven hours."

She read through the email from the school containing the itinerary. "The buses are going to beat us there then. This is taking longer than we thought it would."

"Well, we stopped a bunch of times yesterday."

She gave him an accusatory look. "You mean *you* stopped a bunch of times."

"Hey, you're the one who wanted the waterfall."

"OK, I'll give you that. But if we had driven straight through, we would be there already."

"Probably. But we'd be exhausted, you'd still be falling all over from your concussion—"

She smacked his arm. "Which was *your* fault."

"And the bus wouldn't even be there yet," he continued. "This way, we get there right after they do. It's perfect." He gazed over at her. "And if we hadn't stopped for the night, you wouldn't have a good memory to replace one of the bad ones."

She raised an eyebrow at him. "I don't know about that."

"Well, it was good for me," he chuckled, which earned him another smack on the arm. "I'm gonna come up with more stuff we can do during storms to erase the bad memories."

"Colton." It seemed wrong for him to speak of the future as if they really had one.

"Have you ever slept in a treehouse? I have one back in the woods by my house that my dad had built for me. We could go up there and—"

"I don't need you to fix me," she snapped, wanting him to stop.

"I didn't ... I mean, I wasn't trying to. I just want to help."

She regretted her tone. "I know, but stop talking like there's an *us*. It makes things worse."

"What does that mean?" His emerald eyes left the road and held on her.

"Watch the road." She pointed ahead.

He looked forward again. "Explain."

"I told you last night. You think things are different, but I know what's going to happen once we get to Virginia."

"No, you don't."

"Yes, I do. You're deluding yourself if you think we can have any kind of relationship after we get there. This isn't reality."

He gritted his teeth, and his jaw muscle twitched. "You really tick me off when you start saying negative crap like that."

"I'm being realistic."

"Well, what if I told you I'm not very fond of my reality and haven't been for a long time? What if I told you that you're more real to me than anybody else in my life right now?"

She didn't know how to reply to that.

"So, stop telling me what's going to happen. Because you have no idea."

Natalie stared out the window as Colton cranked the radio volume up too loud. A part of her wondered what it would be like to actually be in a real relationship with him, not just the two-day road trip relationship they were in now.

She took out her phone and noticed a bunch of text notifications from Olivia.

Livvy:
What happened between you and Colton last night?

Natty:
Nothing. Why?

Livvy:
You're such a liar.

Natty:
Why do you say that?

Olivia's next text was a screenshot of a photo from Colton's Snapchat posted early that morning. Natalie's mouth fell open at the picture of her asleep on top of the sleeping bag in the tent. The caption read "Sleeping Beauty."

"What the heck?" She turned the volume down on the radio and held the phone out to Colton, who simply smirked. "Why would you post that?"

He shrugged his shoulders. "It was true."

"You're trying to start drama, aren't you?"

"Maybe."

She grumbled and opened Snapchat to see the post for herself. There were a zillion messages to her account from Lexi and friends demanding she stay away from Colton and calling her every horrible name in the book. This was definitely not what she wanted. They were less than a month away from graduation, and all she wanted was to finish out the year quietly as she had managed to do for the past four years. "You have no idea what you've done, do you? I told you I don't want any trouble with Lexi."

"What's going to happen, really?"

"She and her friends will target me and make the next few weeks unbearable."

"I won't let them."

She rolled her eyes. "You know, I thought there might be a little backlash from coming on this trip with you, but I never expected it to end up like this. I never expected to be back on Lexi's radar again."

"Was it really that bad before?"

"I almost left school. My dad was ready to homeschool me. She and the Hannahs just would not stop. I couldn't walk down the hall without them giving me dirty looks or calling me names or throwing things at me. And whatever pranks you could come up with to do to someone, they came up with worse."

"Such as?"

Natalie would rather forget every horrible thing Lexi had ever done to her, but Colton needed to know who his girlfriend really was. "The worst was when they poured urine all over the inside of my locker."

"What? No way!"

"It was bad. Everything was ruined, including a project for English class I had been working on for weeks."

"Lexi did that?" His shocked expression was enough to assure her that he truly knew nothing about Lexi's pranks. A tiny part of her had worried that he might have had some part in them.

"I could never prove it, and the school wouldn't do anything about it despite a bunch of complaints from my dad. I kept meeting with the counselor to tell her what was happening, and Lexi and her friends would be called in too, and they would act all sweet in front of her, like they loved me and had done nothing wrong. It was pathetic. And in the end, I felt like I brought it on myself or something, or like I was actually making it up like they were saying. It was very confusing. I cried myself to sleep every night, and I cried every morning when I got ready for school."

"I can't believe that. The school should've done more for you."

"I think their no bullying policy can only be enforced when they have actual proof of the bullying. Lexi and her friends were clever, and they never got caught. So, I was screwed."

"I'm sorry you had to go through that."

"I made it through."

"Honestly, when I posted that picture this morning, I wanted to make Lexi mad."

"Why?"

"So I wouldn't have to be the one to break up with her."

Natalie stared at him in silence until he looked at her.

"I've wanted it to be over for a while now."

Her initial feeling of hope at his admission was quickly replaced by anger as the truth sank in. "So, you're using me to get rid of her. Great."

"Not really."

"That's exactly what you're doing." She was fuming. He had gone too far this time.

"So maybe I am. Sort of. So what. Don't you want to help me get her out of my life?"

Colton deserved better, but she couldn't help him with this. And her heart broke a little thinking maybe he didn't really care about her after all. Maybe he only wanted to use her as an excuse to end things with Lexi.

"Why can't you just be honest with her? Being a part of all this makes things worse for me."

"You're right. I'm sorry. I didn't know it would make her post that stuff."

Confusion crossed Natalie's face. "Wait, what did she post?" She flipped her phone over and scrolled down to Lexi's name on her Snapchat list. There was a selfie of her holding someone else's phone showing the Sleeping Beauty picture. She was wearing a devilish expression, her tongue sticking out, her middle finger pointing at the camera. Natalie tapped the screen and a picture from one of her gymnastics meets popped up—most likely acquired from her YouTube channel, where she had posted videos of all her routines for college scouts to see. The caption stated some not very nice things about how Natalie looked in a leotard. She shook her head. "That's just great." It was ridiculous how immature Lexi and the Hannahs still were after all this time.

"I'm sorry." Colton gazed at her with sad puppy dog eyes. "How can I make it up to you?" He reached into the bag of snacks and held a Twizzler out to her, as if that made everything all right.

But he didn't get it. No matter how sorry he was, no matter how he looked at her with those gorgeous eyes of his, it wouldn't change the fact that he had posted that picture. It wouldn't fix things for either of them with Lexi.

She shook her head. "Damage is done."

15
Friends

They rode in silence for a while after that. Natalie didn't know what to say, and she wouldn't know how bad things were until they actually reached their destination. As much as she dreaded facing Lexi, a part of her heart still hurt from the loss of their friendship. They had known each other practically since birth. Lexi's mother and hers had been best friends growing up. They lived two doors down from each other on the cul de sac where Natalie still lived. Their parents spent a lot of time together. So it was inevitable that they would be friends. And they were, for a long time—Natty and Lex, best friends forever.

And then Lexi's mother became ill and the evil cancer took her from them when Lexi was five.

After that, she spent most of her time at their house while her dad worked. Natalie loved having her there. Being an only child, it was like she had a sister. They did everything together, including gymnastics, and the girls spent a lot of time with Natalie's mom— when Mom wasn't having one of her days, that is.

She still wasn't sure exactly why things had changed, but Lexi had suddenly pulled away. She no longer came to their house. She got new friends. She started hanging out with more guys than girls. She quit gymnastics. And the things they'd always had in common, the things that had kept their friendship strong, seemed to slip away overnight.

She lost Lexi. Then her mom split. And then the bullying started.

If it hadn't been for her dad, things might have been worse for her. Their relationship had helped her through the anxiety and depression. She had dealt with so much without a mother around, but she never felt completely alone. Her dad and her faith had gotten her through some of the worst days of her life.

But there were others—like Colton's brother, Chris, and other classmates—who had been ridiculed and picked on, who struggled with depression, who had no support system in place. Others who had chosen to end it all.

Natalie had never reached that point. But with all the mean girl texts that morning, the anxiety monster had begun to rear its ugly head once more. The tight knot in her stomach was back, and the uneasy feeling would not go away. Her usual slow breathing and prayer helped, but it all hung over her like a dark cloud. And it didn't help that it had started to rain again.

She watched the wipers glide back and forth over the windshield.

"I'm sorry." Colton broke the silence. "I know you're mad at me right now."

"I don't appreciate being used. I thought ..." She wasn't sure she should even say it.

"What?"

"I thought we were friends." She couldn't look at him.

"We are." He squeezed her hand.

"I'm just worried about what's going to happen when we get there. I wanted a nice quiet vacation with my friends, and now I have to deal with the wrath of Lexi."

"I'm such an idiot." He wound his fingers through hers. "I'm going to make sure you have the perfect vacation. Trust me, OK?"

She nodded, but she wasn't sure she believed it.

Natalie's phone rang then. "Hey, Liv."

Colton's hand slid away from hers and back to the steering wheel.

"Hey yourself," Olivia replied. "How's it going?"

"Fine."

"Looked like more than fine to me."

"I was asleep. Alone, if you didn't notice." She caught Colton's smirk out of the corner of her eye.

"Yes, but Colton took the picture and posted that cute caption."

"You're reading way too much into things."

"Yeah, well, so is the rest of the school."

The knot in Natalie's stomach squeezed tighter. "Everyone should just mind their own business."

"I didn't mean to upset you," Olivia said.

Natalie hadn't meant to snap. "I'm not mad at you, Liv. I'm glad you told me. It's just, I'm getting all this crap from Lexi and the Hannahs already. It's not good."

"Yeah, she was so ticked that you guys didn't make it to the hotel last night. She was snapping at everyone and complaining loudly about it at the hotel pool. And she keeps asking me if I've heard from you and what's going on with you two. I told her you're just driving to the beach, that's it."

"Thank you. That's the truth."

"I don't think she believed me. Especially after the pictures."

Natalie groaned.

"Is that all there is to it? Really? You can tell me."

"If I could, I would, but we're in the car right now."

"Man, I can't wait until I see you. This sucks, you not being able to tell me what's happening. Can I ask you yes or no questions?"

"No."

"Come on. Pleeease."

"Fine."

"Was it Colton's idea to sleep in the tent?" Olivia asked.

"Yes."

"Did you two sleep together?"

Natalie coughed. "No, of course not."

"I mean, did you sleep together in the sleeping bag?"

"Sort of."

"That's not a yes or no answer."

"I can't elaborate at this time." She spoke as quietly as she could, but there was no hiding her conversation from Colton.

"Did he kiss you?" There was no mistaking the girlish excitement in Olivia's voice.

"Almost."

"What? What do you mean 'almost'?"

"I can't elaborate," she repeated.

"Natalie!"

Natalie couldn't help but laugh at Olivia's reaction. She glanced over at Colton, who was smirking again in that cute way of his. Maybe he could hear Olivia's questions. She *was* talking kind of loud.

"Is he as nice as you always hoped he would be?" Olivia asked.

"Yes." She peered out the window at the passing signs. "Are you on the bus?"

"Yeah, we just left the hotel."

"So how long until you get there?"

"We're supposed to get there at like two o'clock."

They passed a sign for Shanksville just then, and Natalie pointed to it. "Oh man, we should go see the Flight 93 Memorial."

"Next time," Colton replied.

Olivia giggled on the other end of the phone. "Did I hear him right?"

"What did you hear?"

"Did he just tell you *next time* you would go to the Memorial?"

"No."

"Yes, he did. Oh my gosh, what is happening with you two?"

"Stop asking that."

"I'm sorry, but this is like one of those books or movies where the characters get stuck together in some unexpected circumstances and end up falling in love."

"It is not."

"It *so* is."

Natalie rolled her eyes. "I gotta go."

"Call me if anything interesting happens." Olivia giggled.

"Goodbye, Liv."

"Livvy out."

She groaned as she hung up. "Even my best friend is giving me a hard time about us."

He didn't reply.

She noticed him grinning. "What're you grinning at?"

"You said *us*."

"So."

He kept grinning.

Natalie's phone rang again, and she tapped her screen without checking to see who it was. "What now?"

"Hey, Sleeping Beauty," a deep voice answered.

"Who is this?"

"Someone who wants to be your Prince Charming," he replied.

Natalie heard laughter as the guy on the end of the line shushed whoever was with him. "How did you get this number?"

"The only thing that matters is you and me, baby."

She hung up.

"Who was that?" Colton asked.

She didn't reply.

"Who?" He looked concerned.

"I don't know. Some guy messing with me." Her phone rang again. Same number. She tapped "decline", but moments later it rang again.

Colton snatched it from her hand and answered. "Who is this?"

Whoever it was hung up.

He glanced at the screen. "Hey, grab my phone and open up my contacts."

"What for?"

"Just do it."

She did as he asked.

"Scroll down to Grant's name and tell me his number."

She read the number off to him, and of course, it matched.

He tapped her screen to dial the number then put the phone on speaker. It rang three times before the guy picked up.

"Baby." He held out the *e* sound. "I knew you couldn't deny the connection between us." More laughter in the background.

"Grant, this is Colton."

"Oh, man, Colton, that girl is *fine*. Tell me you hit that last night."

Natalie tensed up at his crudeness.

"You're on speaker," Colton replied.

"He put me on speaker," he whispered to his friends, which made them all erupt into more laughter.

Colton rolled his eyes. "You guys are idiots. Stop calling her."

"Take me off speaker," Grant said.

"No way."

"It's about Lexi."

Colton paused as if asking permission from Natalie, who simply shrugged. He pressed the speaker button and put the phone to his ear. "What about her?"

Natalie watched Colton's eyes narrow a little at whatever Grant said to him.

"I'm hanging up now." And he did. He handed the phone back to Natalie. "Sorry about him. About all of them. They really are idiots."

"Is everything OK with Lexi?" she asked.

He rolled his eyes again. "He said she was crying at the hotel last night."

Natalie didn't like being a source of tension between Colton and his girlfriend—even if that girlfriend *was* Lexi. "Maybe you should call her."

"I don't want to deal with her drama right now. I'll talk to her when we get there," he replied.

"If you think that's best."

He glanced over at her. "What, you don't?"

"It sounds like her feelings are hurt."

A look of surprise crossed his face. "Are you seriously worried about her feelings? Even after the horrible way she treated you?"

"Just because someone's wronged me doesn't mean I have to do the same to them. Once upon a time, Lexi was my best friend, and I still care about her. She's obviously hurting over you, and it's because of me, and I feel bad about that."

He shook his head, his eyes narrowing, his forehead scrunching up. "I can't figure you out, Natalie Rhodes."

"I'm a pretty straightforward kind of girl. Not a lot of mystery here. What you see is what you get."

He slowly moved his head from side to side in disbelief. "I think there's a lot more to you than meets the eye."

She shook her head. "Nah."

"One minute you're telling me about being bullied and the next you're so compassionate toward the one who bullied you."

"I try to be kind and follow the Golden Rule—do unto others and all that."

"Don't you just want to hurt her like she hurt you?" he asked.

"I admit, there were times when I wanted to get back at her. But that was my anger getting the better of me. I would never set out to hurt her intentionally."

"Knowing some of the things she did to you back then, knowing what she and her friends have been saying to you since yesterday ... I want nothing to do with her right now."

"She didn't do anything to *you*."

"I don't want to be with someone who's capable of that behavior."

"Really?" She was the one who was surprised this time. "Because you're a part of that group. You all stick together. You laugh when your friends laugh at someone. And when I saw you with Lexi and all your friends standing near my locker that day, laughing, all I could think was that you were all in on it."

He shook his head. "I had nothing to do with any of her pranks on you."

"Guilt by association," she replied. "You've all made someone feel stupid and small. And you've pulled your share of pranks on people without any thought for the person you hurt. I know you have."

"We're just goofing around."

"I'm sure the person you're laughing at doesn't see it that way."

"It's harmless pranks. Stupid little stuff. Not pissing in someone's locker."

"You know bullying is one of the top reasons kids commit suicide, right?" The words were out of her mouth before she could stop them. Her hand came up to cover her mouth, regret overcoming her.

The color drained from his face.

Think before you speak. Her father's words echoed in her mind.

"Colton, I'm so sorry. I didn't mean ..." She wished she could snatch her words back and swallow them down, because the look on his face shattered her heart, and she had put it there.

He stared at the road ahead, jaw tight, muscles in his arms twitching as he gripped the steering wheel.

She really wished she had followed her dad's advice this time.

16
Looking Up

The mood in the car was heavy after that. Off the beaten path they went, through the mountains of Maryland. For a while, they didn't say much. Natalie thought about their conversation over the past hour and she figured that's what Colton was doing too, because he hadn't really spoken either. Maybe he was just trying to pay attention to the wet, winding roads they were traveling on.

They passed through several small towns. Some appeared to be abandoned industrial towns in the middle of the mountains or along rivers. The buildings were old and run down, houses dilapidated, cars beat up. It reminded her of her grandparents'—mom's parents—small town in West Virginia, a mountain town like these with the same rundown buildings and homes. The thought of her mother growing up in that poor little town had always made her sad. She couldn't imagine finding much happiness there. Could that have contributed to her mom's depression? Had either of her grandparents struggled with a mood disorder? If so, could that have something to do with her mom's condition? She knew her mother's depression had to do with messed up serotonin levels in her brain, but the hows and whys remained.

She hadn't let herself think about Mom's absence from her life in a while. But driving through these towns brought her to the forefront of Natalie's mind. She missed her mom. And that little corner of her heart where she had tucked away the memories began to ache.

"I need to pee," Colton announced as he pulled into a tiny gas station on the outskirts of another small town.

"Not in a locker, I hope." She thought maybe it would lighten the mood.

101

He didn't laugh. "Do you have to go?"

"I'm good for now." She was thankful for the reprieve from her thoughts. If she dwelled on Mom for too long, she might sink into the overwhelming sadness she had felt in the early days without her.

Colton returned with a bottled water and a Brisk Raspberry Tea. "It's not Arizona Tea, but it's all they had."

"That's fine. Thanks." She smiled, touched that he remembered what she drank the day before.

"You're welcome."

"I'm sorry, Colton."

He nodded and gave her a weak smile. "I know you didn't mean anything by it."

"I didn't. At all. I would never hurt you on purpose."

He laid his hand over hers. "Forget about it."

On they drove, and with each town they passed, Virginia Beach grew closer and closer. With every mile, reality loomed, and Natalie wished their time together would stretch on and on like the road before them. It was hard for her to believe that they had only been together for a day, that the moment he pulled out in front of her had happened yesterday. Things felt different, like he had said in the tent. It was as if they had stepped into an alternate timeline—away from friends, away from teachers, away from their families, their pasts, their futures. It was just them—driving, talking, moving forward toward something, but what? A destination, yes. Virginia Beach, yes. But it felt like more, like there was something more happening, something important that would change them both forever. Or was that wishful thinking? Was that just her twelve-year crush talking?

Around a bend, the road gave way to a beautiful view of mountains along the river.

"Whoa!" Natalie took out her phone and opened the window to get some pictures of the scene. "That's beautiful."

"Nice," Colton responded. He pointed to a house perched on top of the tallest hill. "Build me a house right up there."

Natalie thought about that for a minute. "I think I'd rather live at the base and be able to look up at the mountain every day."

"You seemed to like looking down from the mountaintop this morning."

"I can't really identify with the guy living up there, though. I'd rather live in a rickety old shack along the river and know who I was and what I believe than live in a mansion up there with no clue, looking down my nose at everyone."

"Wow! That seemed very pointed."

"Just my opinion. I'm allowed to have one of those, right?"

He stared straight ahead. "I could turn that around on you and ask why in the world you would want to live in a house like that ..." He pointed to one of the rundown homes. "... when you could live up there in a nice house with a killer view. Why would you settle for the bottom when you could live on top?"

"Some people aren't settling. It's the hand they're dealt in life. Not everyone can afford the killer view."

"I get that."

Did he? Colton's viewpoint was so different from hers. He wanted to see the world from above—she would never say it, but she was thinking *like a king*—while she wanted to look up at the beauty, look to what was above. And maybe she didn't want the kind of attention Colton was used to, the kind that came from living life like you're above everyone else.

The hum of the tires on the road was the only sound in the car.

"Just out of curiosity, if you could live anywhere in the world, where would you live?" he asked.

Natalie was thankful for the change of subject, and she didn't have to think about her answer. "Italy."

"Why Italy? For the chicken parmesan?"

She smiled and shrugged her shoulders. "I don't know. I've never actually been there, but it looks amazing."

"It is."

Her mouth fell open a little. "You've been to Italy?"

He nodded. "You should go sometime."

"Oh, I could never afford it."

"I'll take you someday." He said it nonchalantly, like they could hop on a plane and go right now if they wanted to.

"No, you won't."

"Sure, I will. Don't you want to go?"

"With you?" She raised an eyebrow at him.

"Of course with me."

"Italy is a major trip, Colton."

He nodded. "We would have so much fun in Italy. We could go to Rome and see the ruins and eat so much spaghetti our stomachs hurt ..." His eyes fixed on her stomach. "Well, maybe not you. Your stomach is a bottomless pit."

She laughed at that.

"We could have pizza in Naples and gelato in Florence, then we'd sail to Capri and eat pasta, swim in the Mediterranean, ride a gondola in Venice and—"

"Eat more pasta." Natalie completed his sentence, giddy at the idea of it.

They laughed.

"Oh my gosh. It all sounds so amazing." She couldn't believe they were talking about Italy or that he was perfectly describing the vacation of her dreams.

"Let's do it." He nodded once as if this was a real trip they were discussing, as if they had actually decided to go.

She took a deep breath in and sighed. "It's nice to dream."

"It doesn't have to be just a dream." He reached over and squeezed her hand.

She wanted to believe that one day it could happen, that they might travel to a place as romantic as Italy. Together. That he would be hers and she would be his. But their time was limited, and once their feet hit that Virginia Beach sand, their little bubble would burst.

17
A Truth Revealed

Natalie stood in front of the mirror at a McDonald's in Fredericksburg, Virginia washing her hands. She looked up at herself and tilted her head from side to side. Her dark hair was wavy from air drying all morning, and she frowned. She twisted it up in a messy bun on top of her head and smiled knowing Colton thought she was cute when she wore it that way.

When she emerged, Colton was seated in a booth waiting for her with their drinks, typing on his phone, looking annoyed.

"Everything OK?" she asked as she took a sip of her strawberry banana smoothie.

He tapped a few more times, then clicked the screen off. "Fine."

"Really?"

"I'm beginning to think we'd have more fun if we didn't make it to Virginia Beach."

Natalie gave him a look. "Right."

"I'm almost serious."

"I couldn't do that. My parents expect me to go there."

"I know." He nodded.

Natalie's phone sounded then with a text. "It's like he knew I was talking about him." She held up the phone and showed Colton a text from her dad asking how she was and how the trip was going.

"Are you going to tell him about us driving down here?" he asked.

"I'll tell him when we get there."

"He'll be mad, won't he?"

"Probably." She opened her phone and stared at the text from her dad then typed a message telling him the trip was going fine and that they would be arriving in a few hours. She laid her phone on the table.

"I'm such a liar."

Colton leaned closer and read her text. "What do you mean? That's not a lie."

"It's a lie by omission. If he knew I was here with you instead of on that bus, he would probably call the cops on us."

His brow furrowed. "Why? You're an adult. You can go anywhere you want without his permission."

She chewed on the inside of her lip. Keeping the truth about the trip from her parents wasn't her only lie of the weekend. "Actually ... I don't turn eighteen until Friday."

"What? Natalie!" Colton had every right to be ticked off, and he was. "I could get into a lot of trouble for bringing a minor across state lines without permission."

"I know. I'm sorry. I should've told you sooner."

He pressed his lips together and shook his head. "You shouldn't have come at all." Colton stood and tossed his empty cup in the trash, leaving her sitting alone.

Natalie didn't know what to say. She hesitantly stood and followed him outside to the car. The rain had slowed to a light sprinkle.

He slammed his car door hard as he got in, and she winced.

She climbed into the silent vehicle and pulled her door closed. "If you want me to call my parents, I will. I don't want to get you into any kind of trouble. I don't know why I lied. I wasn't thinking, and part of me really wanted to go on this trip with you."

He looked over at her. "I don't want you to call them."

"OK." Natalie pursed her lips to fight back tears.

"We're close. Let's just get you there. You can ride home on the bus, and they never have to know."

"I'm still going to tell them." She wanted to be completely honest with him from here on out.

"When you get home?" he asked.

"Probably. I don't know. If Dad calls and asks me a question I have to lie to answer, I'm going to have to come clean."

He nodded. "I get it."

The car remained silent with the engine off.

"Aren't you going to start the car?"

Colton was deep in thought. "What if your parents hate me when they find out the truth?"

"I'm sure they won't hate either of us, but they probably won't be too happy about it. Especially since you're the reason I wrecked my car."

"I mean, what if this affects things." He picked at nothing on his steering wheel.

"What're you talking about?"

"Us." His eyes met hers.

The butterflies went wild in her stomach. "There isn't an us, Colton."

"You never know what might happen in the future."

"What exactly are you saying?" She was anxious to know what he was thinking.

"What if I want to take you out? If they find out we went on this trip together, they might not let me anywhere near you."

Natalie's lips turned up despite her best efforts to keep a straight face. He seemed incredibly insecure at the moment, and she found him adorable.

He shook away his thoughts and turned the key, and the car came to life.

"In three hours, you won't even remember my name," Natalie replied.

"You're funny." Amusement replaced the uncertainty in his eyes.

"It's probably true."

"You should take that sense of humor and do something with it." His eyes lit up. "Ventriloquism, perhaps."

Natalie burst out laughing. "Oh, I miss little Davey."

"I'm sure he misses you too." The mood lightened as he shifted the car into reverse and headed out on the last stretch of their journey.

As they moved closer to their destination, the skies grew dark and stormy, which put Natalie on edge. "Do you think we'll get stuck driving in that? Maybe it will pass us by."

He shook his head. "The clouds pretty much wrap around us. I don't think we can avoid it." He laid his hand on her knee and squeezed. "We'll be fine."

A jolt of electricity shot up her leg.

She was about to respond when Colton suddenly swerved the car. "Whoa!" he cried.

Whatever he had tried to avoid, went under his right front tire causing them to bounce roughly over it.

"What was that?" she asked.

"Something metal. I'm not sure. It better not have put a hole in my—" The sudden *thump, thump, thump* of the tire stopped Colton mid-sentence. "Crap!"

He maneuvered the vehicle carefully to the shoulder and smacked his palm against the steering wheel. "I *just* put new tires on this a month ago."

"Do you have a spare?"

"Yeah, there's a full-size spare back there." He grumbled as he turned off the ignition and looked back over his shoulder toward the highway before opening his door.

Natalie joined him next to the front tire. "It's flat."

That got a chuckle out of Colton. "Thanks. I didn't know." He stood staring at it.

"Shouldn't you get out your jack?" She nodded toward the rear of his car.

"Yeah." He moved toward the trunk and removed the jack.

Natalie watched as he set it under the car and fiddled with the bar that attached to it, then started turning it.

"You have to loosen the lug nuts before you raise the car," she told him.

"Right." He used the lug wrench to loosen them, then returned to raising the car.

His technique was slow and awkward.

"You *have* changed a tire before, right?" she asked.

He shrugged his shoulders in reply.

"You haven't? Oh my gosh. I've finally found something that Colton Daynes can't do."

"I can do it," he snapped.

"So can I."

Colton's eyebrow raised. "Really?"

She bumped his hip with hers. "Let me show you how it's done."

And she took over removing the damaged tire and replacing it with the spare, lowering the vehicle, and tightening the lug nuts. "Ta da!"

He sidled up next to her. "That was kind of hot."

She smacked his arm. "How have you never changed a tire?"

"When would I ever have a reason to? I've never had a flat before."

"I haven't either, but my dad taught me how so I would know in case of a situation like this." And, boy, was she thankful for that at this moment.

"Your dad sounds like a really great guy."

"He is. He's the best."

"I doubt my dad even knows how to change a tire. And if he had a flat, he'd pay someone to change it for him."

It saddened Natalie that he didn't have a good relationship with his father and that nobody had taught him skills like this, skills every driver should know.

"What else can you do?" Colton asked.

"I can change the oil, replace all the fluids, change the air filter, change my wipers. Simple stuff, really."

"*Mhmm*. Real simple."

"Most of it is. And my Honda is an older year, so it's good for me to know this stuff." She screwed up her face. "I wonder if I'll be able to get it fixed or if it's totaled. I need that car to get me to college."

"If it's totaled, I'll help you buy a new one."

Her mouth dropped open. "Col—"

"Don't even try to stop me. I owe you after you changed my tire."

A little snort escaped her. "Because twenty minutes spent changing a tire is worth the cost of a car."

He dangled his keys in front of her. "I think you've also earned the right to drive the rest of the way."

"Really?" His car really did drive like a dream.

"Absolutely."

She reached for the keys, and he held them above her head.

"Hey!"

He laughed aloud, and handed them over.

The sound of a car pulling up behind them grabbed their attention. They both froze like deer in headlights as a Virginia state trooper stepped from his car and approached them.

"Everything OK here?" the officer asked.

"Flat tire," Colton replied. "We're just finishing up."

Natalie wondered if he was as nervous as she was, but he kept his cool and went about taking care of the jack and wrench. She tried not to show her nerves, but she was sweating and the sound of the approaching storm was getting to her as well. A sudden boom of thunder caused her to jump and let out a yelp.

"Are you all right, miss?" The officer moved closer to her.

"Oh, I'm fine." She rested her hand over her heart. "I just don't like storms, that's all. The thunder freaks me out."

"It should blow through in the next fifteen minutes or so. If you keep heading south, you should drive out of it in no time."

"Oh, thank you." She let out a sigh.

"Where you headed?" the officer asked.

"Virginia Beach," Natalie answered.

"Just the two of you?" He glanced over at Colton.

"For a school trip," she answered, afraid to give away too much information.

"Where's the rest of your class?" he asked.

"On the bus. We had to drive separately because of a ... scheduling conflict."

The officer nodded. "Well, safe travels to you."

"Thanks for checking on us." Colton closed the trunk and nodded at the man.

Natalie tried to act casual as she climbed back into the passenger side of the car.

Colton waited by the rear of the car for a few vehicles to pass before walking to the driver's side and taking his place behind the wheel. His hands were visibly shaking, as were Natalie's as she held the keys out to him. "I thought you were going to drive."

"I forgot." She was too flustered to care.

He took the keys from her and fired up the engine, cautiously driving onto the highway and keeping his speed just under the limit.

Natalie stared in the side mirror at the trooper driving behind them. "Do you think he's checking your plates or something?"

"I don't know." He gripped the steering wheel tightly.

"What if he pulls us over? He's going to ask for licenses."

"Relax, Natalie. You're starting to freak me out." Colton activated the wipers as the rain began to fall.

A couple miles down the road, the officer was still tailing them. Colton kept his speed in check, his eyes constantly bouncing between the road and the rearview mirror.

"Don't you think if he was going to stop us, he would've done it by now?" Natalie asked.

The lights on top of the police car suddenly began flashing as if in answer to her question.

"Oh, no!" Natalie eyes shot to Colton's, her heart in her throat.

"Are you kidding me?" He slowed down and began to pull off the road.

"We're so busted." Tears burned Natalie's eyes. "I'm so sorry, Colton. This is all my fault. I don't want you to go to jail."

The police car suddenly went speeding past them, sirens blaring.

Colton let out a deep breath as he pulled back onto the road and drove on. "Must've had something more urgent."

Natalie inhaled deeply through her nose as her head fell back against the seat. "Oh my gosh!" She exhaled the words.

"Man, I'm gonna be glad when we get there," he said.

She nodded in agreement.

Colton shook his head as he looked over at her. "'Oh, Colton, I don't want you to go to jail.'" He mocked her earlier freak-out.

"Hey, I was really worried." She crossed her arms over her chest.

He busted up laughing, and she couldn't help but laugh along with him.

"Did you want to drive?" he asked.

Natalie motioned toward the dark clouds ahead. "No, thanks."

And it was as if the clouds sensed her fear, because they burst open at that moment and began dumping rain down on them. Colton slowed the car to a crawl when it became nearly impossible to see the road ahead.

Natalie distracted herself by thinking about last night's storm and how Colton had helped her through it. Her stomach flipped as she remembered the way he held her and sang with that smooth voice of his. No matter what happened when they reached Virginia Beach, even if they never spoke again, she would always have those memories.

The rain grew heavier.

"I have to pull off. I can't see the road at all." He steered slowly to the side behind other cars that were stopped and activated his hazard lights.

Natalie was shaking. "This is horrible."

And it only grew worse as little hail stones began pelting the vehicles and bouncing off.

"Oh, that better not leave marks," Colton warned as if the clouds would hear him and stop.

Lightning flashed and thunder boomed almost simultaneously, making it known that they were sitting directly in the center of the storm.

Tears burned Natalie's eyes. "Colton," she whimpered.

"Hey." He took her hand in his.

"Why are there so many storms on this trip?" She gripped his forearm with her other hand.

"We'll get through them, Natalie. We'll get through them all."

She was trembling then as a bolt of lightning struck close by and thunder clapped. A scream escaped her, and she squeezed her eyes closed to shut it all out. She suddenly felt a hand smooth across her cheek, gently turning her head, then warm breath against her face just before soft lips met hers for a single perfect kiss.

Her eyes flew open to Colton's face hovering close to hers, those green eyes fixed on her lips. He leaned in again and brushed his full lower lip against her upper one, and she responded, kissing him softly once, twice, three times. He took her face in both hands as they kissed again. She lost count of how many times after that as the kisses grew longer and they became more wrapped up in each other. She gripped his forearms, and shivers, which were in no way related to the storm outside, traveled her entire body. Natalie knew she would never think of lightning and thunder the same way again.

Colton pressed one final soft kiss to her lips before resting his forehead against hers. "Feel better?"

She couldn't find the words, so she simply nodded and let go of his arms as his hands slipped from her face.

"Good." He sat back in his seat.

"That ..." She swallowed through the nerves and the still very active butterflies in her stomach. "That was just to distract me, right?"

He gave her a goofy grin. "Of course."

"That's what I thought."

"And because I've wanted to kiss you since you hid under my sweatshirt at the gas station."

Her lips curved to one side. "Not my best moment."

"You were cute. And nobody's ever said that to me before."

"Said what?"

"That they couldn't be seen with me. People usually *want* to be seen with me."

She formed an *O* with her lips. "Well, aren't you hot stuff?"

He shrugged his shoulders. "People seem to think so."

"I just didn't want to get into trouble with my parents for going on this trip with you," she explained. "That's why I said it."

"I know."

"I like being with you because of who you are, Colton. Not because I want to be seen with you."

"You like me." He tilted his head, and his lips turned up in a sweet smile.

"I mean, you're tolerable." She turned away nervously.

"Uh-huh." He laughed. "Those kisses were a dead giveaway."

"How do you know I wasn't thinking about someone else the whole time?" she asked.

"Were you?" He raised an eyebrow at her.

She angled her head and smiled.

"Well, maybe we should try again." He leaned toward her, his gaze fixed on her mouth. "I can make you think about me and only me."

She pressed her hand against his chest to stop his advance.

"No?" His eyebrows raised in question.

She shook her head. "No."

Colton turned away and fiddled with the air conditioner controls. "Is it hot in here?"

She giggled.

He glanced over at her, then leaned back in his seat. "An enigma, I tell ya."

"An enigma?"

"You're hard to figure out."

"I didn't know you knew the word *enigma*."

His eyes narrowed. "I'm not the dumb jock everyone thinks I am."

"I didn't say you were dumb."

"I'm tired of being judged because I like sports and drive a nice car."

"Hey, I'm not judging you." A little laugh escaped her. "I was teasing. Don't dish it out if you can't take it."

He sat quiet for a minute. "I'm sorry. I didn't mean to snap. It's getting more and more annoying to deal with that kind of stuff lately. Most times, people are serious. I wouldn't have been accepted to MSU with bad grades, but people don't get that. They think daddy bought my way in. But I earned this, whether or not our name got me in there."

"You know you're always going to deal with judge-y people, right? Everyone has to deal with them at some point in their life. But as long as you know the truth, that's all that really matters."

He nodded.

"And I'm not completely innocent," she admitted. "I've watched you and listened to what other people said about you and made assumptions and judgments without all the facts, without really knowing you, and I'm sorry for that."

"But you know me now. You know the truth about me."

She smiled. "I think I do."

"Then that's all that matters."

18
Life's Path

I f Natalie never heard another rap song in her life it would be too soon. But if listening to rap meant staying in the Camaro with Colton, she would gladly endure it.

"I'm not sure I want to go to MSU," he blurted twenty minutes after the end of their last conversation.

Natalie was taken aback. "But you said you worked so hard to get in there."

"It's a great school, and I know what a big deal a football scholarship is."

"But?" She anxiously awaited what he would say next.

"Sometimes I feel like I'm meant to do something else," he admitted.

"Like what?"

"I don't know. Never mind."

"Don't do that." She feared a repeat of their earlier conversation at the campground. "You've obviously been sitting here thinking about all of this, and you wouldn't have said something if you didn't want to talk about it, so spill."

"I've been thinking about going on a mission trip after graduation."

"A mission trip? Like with a church?" This was not what she expected him to say.

Colton nodded.

"What church?"

"Neil's."

"I thought you didn't go to church," she said.

"I don't."

"O-*kay*." Natalie was confused.

115

"I used to go with Neil sometimes when I was younger, but not after Chris."

"Oh." That was understandable.

"I went with them in November for the first time in three years, and Neil invited me to go on the mission trip this summer with him and Heather to build homes in Guatemala."

"That sounds like a great experience."

"That's what I was thinking. Ever since he asked me, it's been hanging out in my brain, and I can't stop thinking about it. Helping people who don't have homes just feels right. Like, I think I really want to go." There was a fire in his eyes that revealed his longing to do something important and meaningful.

"You can do that and still go to college in the fall, so why are you really unsure about MSU?"

"I just ... I'm feeling a little lost right now, I guess. I'm confused about a lot of things in my life."

"Huh." She shook her head.

"Huh, what?"

"I never would've known you were questioning your future plans."

"Don't you ever do that?" he asked.

"Sometimes, but I always thought you were set for life. Football scholarship, beautiful girlfriend, perfect future all mapped out for you."

"That's the thing, though. I don't want it all mapped out for me." Colton sat up straighter in his seat as he spoke more passionately. "I want to figure it out on my own. I want to know that the path I'm on is one that I chose. Maybe I'll fail, but how will I know unless I try something, something not planned out by my father, ya know?"

She suddenly had a strange thought. "You're a little like Davey."

Colton's brow furrowed. "The ventriloquist dummy?"

"Yeah."

"Gee, thanks." He made a silly face at her.

She giggled. "People speaking for you, I mean. It's like you're speaking for yourself, but there's actually somebody else there behind you, making you do what they want you to do."

"Nice analogy."

"Thanks." She winked.

116

His eyes sparkled when he smiled at her. "And now I know you're more than just the gymnast."

She had nearly forgotten. "Yeah, why did you say that before?"

"Say what?"

"When I told you I liked gymnastics, you said, 'Oh right, you're the gymnast'. What did you mean by that?"

"I don't think I should say." He picked up the napkin-wrapped silverware from the table and ripped apart the paper band that held it all together. His knife dropped with a *clank* to the table.

"Why not?" she asked, clearly puzzled.

"Because you might take back what you just said and realize you were right about me from the start."

"I doubt that."

Colton laid the silverware on top of the napkin, sipped his water, and scanned the restaurant, not making eye contact with her.

"Colton, what?"

"We rate girls." He still wouldn't look at her. "A lot of times we have no idea what their names are, so we give them nicknames."

"Rate them on what?"

He shook his head. "It's not important."

She tilted her head and gave him her best disapproving look. "Just tell me."

His eyes finally met hers. "By how doable they are." He cringed as he said it.

Her mouth dropped open in disgust. "Colton, that's sick and wrong."

He nodded. She could see he was actually ashamed by it, so she didn't say more.

There was a long minute of silence.

"How did I rate?" she asked.

The corner of Colton's mouth turned up a little.

"Never mind." She waved her hands in front of her. "Forget I asked."

He chuckled.

The waitress arrived then with their food.

Colton held up his glass of water toward Natalie. "To a great trip."

Natalie held hers up. "To friendship."

"Are you one-hundred percent sure about Arizona State?" he asked.

"Yes." She had no hesitations whatsoever.

"Why?"

"It's been a dream of mine to compete gymnastics in college. They have a great gymnastics team and a great school. Olivia and I have always talked about going to the same college and rooming together, and that's what we're going to do."

"Did she get a scholarship too?"

"Not a gymnastics one, but she got a couple academic ones and an art scholarship."

"What are you majoring in?" he asked.

"I'm going to study kinesiology so one day I can coach gymnastics."

"Kinesi-what?"

Natalie laughed. "Kinesiology. It's the study of the movement of the body."

"See, you know what you want, and you're headed in the right direction. I don't even know what I want to study. My dad says Business Management so I can follow in his footsteps."

"And you aren't interested in anything else?"

"Sports Medicine has crossed my mind before. Especially after all the concussions I've had playing football."

"It sounds like you really have a heart for helping people."

"I don't know." He shrugged. "Maybe."

It seemed so obvious to her—Guatemala and now this—even if he wasn't so sure yet. "It's worth doing a little research to see if it's something you might want to do."

"My dad believes in making a plan and sticking to it. He'd go nuts if I told him I was starting school with an undeclared major."

Her heart went out to him. "Can't you just be honest and tell him what you want to do?"

"You don't understand."

She laid her hand on his. "Then make me understand."

He turned his hand over and gripped hers. "My dad has been drilling these plans into me since I was a little boy. Get a scholarship to MSU. Take over the family business. It's what he did. It's what his father did. What his grandfather did. It's the family legacy. Not so easy to turn my back on that."

"It's *your* life, Colton. *Your* scholarship. You don't have to depend on him to pay for school. *You* can decide what you study. Not him." She squeezed his hand before letting go.

"I don't know. Other than sports, my dad and I have nothing in common. And we don't talk, not like you do with your dad. He would never understand."

It saddened her that he had no relationship with his dad. She couldn't imagine that, and it made her heart ache with regret for having been dishonest with hers.

"I'm sorry. I wish I could help," she said.

"You already have." He smiled over at her. "I never have anyone to talk to about this stuff."

"Well, you can talk to me anytime you need to. I'm here for you."

"I like you, Natalie Rhodes."

"I know." She grinned.

"I wish we'd stayed friends since that day on the playground."

"Me too."

19
To Us

They were within an hour of their destination when Colton poi[nted] to a sign ahead for a restaurant. "Would you mind if I took [you] out to lunch?"

"We can wait until we get there, Colton. You've bought m[e] many meals already."

"I know, but this'll be our last road trip meal together." A flick[er of] sadness crossed his face.

She smiled at him. "I'd like that."

A grin took the place of his sad expression. "Good."

He took her to a little seafood place, where the waitress se[ated] them in a booth in a quiet corner.

"I'm really glad you came with me," Colton said after they pl[aced] their order.

"So am I. I didn't know what to expect, and I was honestly ki[nd of] nervous."

"Because of my bad driving?"

"Because you're Colton Daynes."

He rolled his eyes. "What, you were intimidated by m[e or] something?"

"Of course. Who wouldn't be?"

Disbelief crossed his face. "You didn't seem to care about w[ho I] was at all when we started this trip."

"I didn't want you to think I was nervous. I tried to pretend [I was] cool and chill about the whole thing."

Colton laughed. "Well, I bought it. You're a good actress."

"But now I know I was wrong about you," she said. "There's [more] to you than just your reputation."

He gazed into her eyes. "To us."

She swallowed hard as he clinked his glass against hers.

The ringer on Colton's phone went off then. He tapped "ignore".

"Lexi?" Natalie asked.

He nodded.

"You can answer it if you want to."

"I'm having lunch with you right now. Everybody else can wait."

That warmed her heart, but it didn't take away her underlying guilt for kissing another girl's boyfriend.

"So, what's the first thing you're going to do when we get there?" he asked. "Besides find your friends and your room."

"Get me to the beach. And fast," she replied with excitement. "I've never been to the ocean before."

"What?" His eyes widened, and he stared at her dumbfounded. "How has this not come up yet?"

She shrugged. "I don't know. We've never really had much extra money for vacations. That's why this trip is so important to me." *No extra money for vacations was more like it.* Day trips to Lake Michigan and gymnastics meets in Ohio, Indiana, and Illinois had been the extent of her travel so far. Virginia Beach was the farthest she had ever been away from home.

"Oh, man, I want to see your face the first time you step into the ocean." He seemed more excited about it than she did.

"Well, you'll be back with your friends by then, and I'll be back with mine," she replied. "I'll send you a video."

This seemed to disappoint him. "Do you have any big plans with your friends this week?"

"We're going on the day trip to Jamestown. The rest of the time, I'll be happy sitting on the beach."

"I probably won't leave the beach very much. Just to eat and sleep."

"Sounds good to me." She grew quiet thinking about Colton off with Lexi and his friends while she, Olivia, and Trinity ventured off to learn about history. Would their paths ever cross this week? She doubted it, and that tugged at her heart and filled her with a dread she hadn't anticipated.

"I really want to hang out with you this week, Nat." Colton must have been thinking about their situation too.

"We'll see." It was all she could think to say in response. In less than an hour, they would arrive at the resort. Then what? An uneasiness settled in. She just didn't see how this could work.

20
Virginia Beach

O h, I don't know about this." Colton gripped the steering wheel as they approached the Hampton Roads Bridge Tunnel leading toward Virginia Beach.

Natalie laughed. "What? Afraid the tunnel's going to fill with water or something?"

"Don't say that," he snapped.

He seemed legitimately worried as they drove through the underwater tunnel, but Natalie couldn't hold in her laughter. "I'm sorry. I just didn't think you were scared of anything."

"I'm not scared." His white knuckles said otherwise.

"Right."

"I'm *concerned* for your safety. We've made it this far. I would hate for something to happen to you now."

"I see." She tried to stifle another laugh.

He let out a breath when they finally emerged on the other side, and Natalie giggled.

"Whatever. You're afraid of storms."

Her attention was no longer on Colton or his jab. She was enamored by the sight of the bay all around them. She couldn't wait to get to the Atlantic and step into the salty waves.

When they arrived at Vacation Villa Resort, Natalie texted Olivia, who informed her that they had hit some construction and were running about an hour behind schedule.

Colton parked in the resort parking lot and got out of his car.

They were in Virginia Beach. They had survived the journey together. And now they would go their separate ways.

Natalie's door suddenly opened, and Colton extended his hand to her. She didn't want to get out. She wanted him to get back in the car and drive them away from there. Together.

"We made it!" he cried.

She nodded and reluctantly took his hand, letting him help her out of the car. "And it only took us, like, eighteen hours of driving."

"Only." With a wink and a smile, he wound his fingers through hers and angled his head toward the beach. "Let's take a walk."

"OK." The sound of the waves against the shore and the smell of the salt in the air filled her with anticipation. She could barely contain her excitement as they walked alongside the resort, anxious to see the massive body of water with her own eyes.

When they rounded the corner of the building, Natalie stopped.

"Oh my goodness!"

She let go of Colton's hand and walked swiftly down the pathway that led to the beach. Her pace slowed as she kicked off her shoes and savored the feeling of soft sand squishing between her toes. She looked over her shoulder, and he was watching her with amusement.

"Race ya!" Natalie's eyes sparkled as she gave him a little push and took off across the sand.

Colton chased after her, their laughter floating on the wind.

When Natalie's feet touched the smooth wet sand, she ran a little harder and did a cartwheel, then proceeded to stand on her hands and walk along the beach that way.

Colton grabbed hold of her ankle, and she screamed. "Stop! You're gonna make me fall!"

"Come on!" He kicked off his shoes and walked calf-deep into the water.

She righted herself and followed him, taking her first steps into the ocean. Her smile was probably the biggest she had ever worn. And when she looked at Colton, he was grinning right back at her.

"It's freezing." She kicked a little water in his direction.

He returned the favor, so she did it again.

And the cycle continued until they were both soaked from head to toe.

Colton stopped splashing and moved closer to her, both of them still laughing. He reached out and moved a wet strand of hair from her forehead.

The sensation of his fingertips gliding against her wet forehead gave her goosebumps on top of the goosebumps she already had from the cold water.

He stepped closer, his hands moving around her waist, pulling her into him.

"Colton," she warned.

He hugged her. So tight she felt like crying.

She locked her arms around his back and leaned her head against his chest, knowing their moments together were fleeting.

"I'm so glad I got to see that," he whispered.

She leaned back, and their eyes met. The way he was looking at her brought back the kiss they had shared only hours before.

It was more than just friendship between them now. She knew better than to say it wasn't. It was more than those secret feelings she had harbored for him since childhood. Because she didn't know him before, and there had never been a chance of anything real happening between them.

This trip had changed all that.

She had totally fallen for him.

And now she was about to lose him.

21
Back to Reality

Rivulets of water slid from Colton's hair down his cheeks and neck, some dripping into the trunk as he retrieved his beach towel. He wiped them away and rubbed back and forth over his hair, leaving it sticking up in every direction, which Natalie found adorable.

He caught her watching him. "What?"

She straightened her face to hide the smile he had seen. "Your hair."

"Oh." He combed through it with his fingers and it righted itself.

She wished she could do the same with hers. Guys had it so easy.

Colton walked over and wrapped his towel around behind her shoulders.

"I have my own towel in there, you know?" She nodded toward the trunk.

"You can use mine. I don't mind."

"I need to get out of these wet clothes." As soon as the words left her mouth, she figured he'd have some smart comment to add, but he only smirked.

The sound of a bus entering the resort parking lot captured their attention.

Natalie couldn't believe it. The buses had finally arrived, but she wasn't sure whether to feel happy or sad. A little of both swirled around inside her.

Colton took her hand and squeezed. Confused emerald eyes gazed at her. His brow furrowed, and his bottom lip stuck out a little in a pout, perfectly displaying the sadness she too felt that their trip was over.

As the bus doors opened and students began filtering out, Colton removed Natalie's bags from his trunk.

"Thanks," she said.

"No problem. I'm glad you came along with me."

"It was fun." She managed to smile through the mix of emotions she was experiencing.

"It had its moments." He smiled and showed her his dimple once more.

"Well, looky what we have here!" A loud, cocky voice hollered from across the parking lot.

Colton looked over his shoulder at his friends.

"Old King Cole!" Grant called.

Natalie saw Colton wince at the nickname, and she gasped.

Colton turned his head toward her.

"What the heck?" She couldn't believe what she had heard. "Why would he call you that?"

"He always does."

Her eyes narrowed. "And you never told him not to?"

"He's been calling me that since we were kids."

A lightbulb went off. "That's why he texted OKC yesterday."

"Yep."

"You didn't tell him about your brother's letter?"

"I told you nobody else knows about the letter. Grant and I don't really talk about serious stuff like that."

"Well, I'm going to tell him to stop." She squared her shoulders, ready for a confrontation.

Colton touched her arm. "Don't. It's easier not to say anything."

Her shoulders sank. She wanted more than anything to put Grant in his place, but she kept quiet as he and a few of the other guys reached them.

"We missed you, dude." Grant's brown eyes met Natalie's for a brief second, then returned to Colton's. "Glad to have you back." He wrapped one arm around Colton's shoulder and rubbed his wet head with the other.

Colton pushed him away.

Grant turned and opened his arms to Natalie, who just stared at him with a smirk.

"Denied," one of the guys said.

The others laughed.

"My hugs are pretty epic, if I do say so myself." Grant tilted his head, his deep brown hair falling to the side, and raised his eyebrows at her.

"Is that so?" Natalie asked.

He opened his arms wider. "I could rock your world if you let me."

"With a hug?" He really was full of himself.

"You know it."

"I'll pass." Natalie heard Colton let out a little laugh.

"COLTON!" Lexi's high-pitched squeal made Natalie cringe.

He didn't seem to notice her—or maybe he chose to ignore her—and turned to Natalie. "Can I carry your bags to your room?"

She shook her head as she laid his towel over the edge of his trunk. "I can manage." She took one bag from him and slid the straps over her shoulder.

"Are you sure?" His eyes almost appeared to be pleading with her.

She gave him a weak smile. "I'm sure."

Natalie slung another bag and her purse over her left arm and lifted the handle on her suitcase. Just as she was about to walk toward the buses, Lexi ran past, nearly knocking Natalie over on her way to Colton.

Lexi jumped onto Colton, wrapping her arms and legs around him. He dropped his bag, arms locking around her back to hold her up, and then they kissed. Colton kissed Lexi—and not just a quick peck, but an open-mouth kiss that seemed to go on forever.

To be fair, Lexi planted the kiss on him first. But even so, Natalie thought she might die of humiliation for having witnessed it up close and personal, for believing him when he said he wanted to break up with Lexi, and for falling for a guy who already had a girlfriend.

When he finally pulled his lips away from Lexi's, his eyes instantly searched for and found Natalie's.

She didn't react, simply stared at him for a few long moments, then turned and walked on toward the buses.

It was over. They were back to reality, just as she said they would be.

"Thanks for keeping him company on the trip," Lexi called after her.

She peeked over her shoulder, taken aback at the comment as Lexi walked toward her.

"I was so worried when I heard he was driving by himself. I'm glad you were there to keep him from falling asleep and ending up in a ditch somewhere."

"Uh …" She wasn't quite sure whether Lexi was being sincere or not. "Yeah. We made it safe and sound."

Lexi suddenly grabbed hold of her shoulder and turned her around, pulling her into a hug. "You're the best."

Natalie felt as if she had exited the vehicle into an alternate reality. This was the nicest Lexi had been to her since before they weren't friends anymore.

Lexi let go, brushing off her shirt as if she could wipe away the water spots left by Natalie's damp clothes. "You should come hang out with us at the beach later."

"Uh … I better go find my friends." She pointed toward the bus.

"OK. See ya later." Lexi bounced across the parking lot, wrapping herself around Colton once again.

Natalie resumed walking and noticed a redhead exiting the second bus. *Trinity*. Sudden unexpected tears sprang to her eyes as Olivia stepped off the bus after her, and she brushed them away before anyone saw.

"Natty!" Olivia and Trinity cried simultaneously. The three girls came together in a group hug.

"Why are you soaking wet?" Olivia stepped back and pulled her now wet shirt away from her skin.

"The ocean." Natalie ached to be standing in the chilly water again, blissed out in Colton's warm embrace.

Trinity didn't seem to care about the state of Natalie's attire. "We missed you. It wasn't the same on the bus without you. And we want to hear every detail."

"Yeah, how was your trip?" Olivia's eyes looked past Natalie and scanned the crowd. "Where is he?"

"Who?" Natalie asked, knowing full well who she was talking about.

Olivia raised an eyebrow at her and shifted her hip in that sassy way of hers when she caught sight of Colton. "Why is he still with *her*?"

Natalie didn't want to look. It was too much. "She's his girlfriend."

"Come on." Trinity headed toward the chaperones. "Let's go find our room. Then you can tell us everything."

"I have a little news of my own," Olivia added.

Natalie raised an eyebrow at her. "Oh?"

The girls joined up with Ms. Heath to get their room assignment.

"Nice of you to join us, Natalie." Ms. Heath gave her a kind smile. "I was worried when your stepmother told me about your accident, but I'm happy you weren't hurt."

"Norma ... you ... you talked to Norma?" Natalie stuttered.

Ms. Heath nodded. "I did. Colton called to tell me the two of you were driving down on your own, so I had to call your parents to confirm."

Natalie's throat tightened as she forced a nod.

"She told me you were late because of the accident, so you caught a ride with him. I hope he drove responsibly."

"He did. Absolutely. All the way. He never sped once, and we took turns driving and stopped to rest." Natalie couldn't stop herself from rambling on, nervous about Ms. Heath's conversation with Norma. There was no way Norma told her about the road trip because neither she nor Dad knew. When Ms. Heath asked if Natalie was riding with Colton, Norma probably thought she meant riding *to the school*, not all the way to Virginia.

"Well, I'm glad you made it safely." Ms. Heath checked the girls' names off her list and held out their room keys.

"Thanks," Natalie replied.

Trinity nearly knocked the keys out of Ms. Heath's hand in a rush to grab them.

"Have fun, girls." Ms. Heath chuckled.

Natalie couldn't walk away fast enough. She was thankful for the miscommunication between Norma and Ms. Heath, but guilt and the fear of getting caught ate away at her.

The loud, obnoxious laughter of Lexi and the Hannahs drew her attention long enough to turn her focus in their direction and notice Colton watching her. Her heart ached when his lips curved into a smile. All she could do was turn away and focus on her girls.

They found their room on the ninth floor, and Olivia and Trinity squealed with delight at the view of the ocean. Natalie couldn't seem to muster as much enthusiasm.

"Oh my gosh! Can you believe it? We totally lucked out." Olivia tugged the sliding door to their balcony open and walked through, the salty air blowing into the room and rippling the sheer curtain.

Natalie took a deep breath. She was finally here. With her girls. She was supposed to be happy about it, but everything felt off. She thought she would arrive and be ecstatic to relax and celebrate the end of their senior year. One last hurrah together. But instead she found herself fighting back tears.

"There's Colton." Olivia called back over her shoulder.

Trinity joined her. "Where?"

"By the pool." She pointed downward then looked back at Natalie. "Lexi's not with him."

But Natalie didn't move, and she finally let the tears flow.

Olivia noticed. "Oh, Natty, what's wrong?" She walked over and wrapped her arms tightly around her friend.

Trinity did the same.

Natalie's shoulders shook as she let it all out. "I don't know why I'm crying like this," she murmured. "I knew it was just a road trip thing."

Olivia let go and looked Natalie in the eyes. "What exactly happened between you two?"

"We kissed," she admitted.

"Seriously?" Trinity grabbed her arm and tugged her over to sit on the bed. "Is he a good kisser?"

Natalie tried to hold back her smile. "It's more than the kiss, you guys. We became friends."

"That's a good thing, isn't it?" Olivia flipped her light brown hair over her shoulder.

"I thought it was. I'm not sure how things are supposed to work now. I mean, he has this whole group of friends and Lexi, and there's no room for me in his world." She had known this was what would happen, but she kept remembering what he said. *You're more real to me than anyone else in my life right now.*

"You don't want to be part of that group anyway, do you?"

She shook her head. "Absolutely not."

"You don't need their permission to be his friend," Trinity interjected.

"I just don't want the last of our high school year ruined by Lexi and her friends. You guys should've read the messages they were sending me. It was like middle school all over again."

"You don't think your relationship is worth a little fallout?" Olivia asked.

A series of images from the past eighteen hours came flooding back—holding hands by the falls, waking in his arms with his fingers in her hair, kissing in the car, hugging in the ocean. Her heart squeezed. "He's worth it."

"Then screw Lexi and her minions."

"Yeah!" Trinity raised a fist in the air.

Natalie giggled. "I'm so glad we're here together. I love you both so much."

"We love you too." Olivia pulled her into another hug.

Natalie sat back and wiped at her face, her thoughts turning again to their moments by the waterfall. "He's different, you guys. Different than I thought he was going to be."

"How so?" Olivia asked.

"He acts tough, like he has it all together, but he has a sensitive side too. He's been through so much and is still going through a lot, and I really want to be there for him, but I'm not sure how."

Olivia rested her arm across Natalie's shoulders. "It's all gonna work out."

"I hope so." Natalie took in a deep breath then exhaled and shook off the lingering tears. "OK, let's go swimming or something. I can't think about this anymore."

"Sounds like a great idea!" Trinity jumped up from the bed and ran off to change. "To the beach!" her voice carried from the bathroom.

Natalie hoped beyond hope that she would not run into Colton and his friends, that maybe they would stay by the pool for the rest of the evening. Because as much as she longed to be near him, she wasn't sure how to act now.

The girls headed out, found an empty spot on the sand for their blanket and towels, and undressed to go swimming. As Natalie removed her shirt, she saw Colton walking in their direction with Grant and their buddies. His eyes were not fixed on her face, and she blushed, suddenly questioning the two-piece swimsuit.

Grant and the others ran past them without acknowledgment, which Natalie was thankful for, but Colton's steps slowed as he neared.

"Hey," he said.

"Hi."

"How *are* you?" His gaze was filled with compassion, apology, and a hint of confusion.

"Fine." She wished that wasn't a lie.

"How's your room?"

"Good." Oh, how she hated awkward small talk.

His eyes remained fixed on hers, and she wished he would look away, because her stomach was fluttering at the intensity she saw there.

"We have an ocean view," she managed to say.

"Us too."

"Nice."

Grant hollered for Colton.

"I, uh ... I gotta go."

"Then go." It came out with more bite than she meant it to, and her eyes rolled as she turned toward her friends.

Olivia and Trinity kept their eyes on Colton.

"Hey." He reached out and brushed the side of Natalie's arm.

Every hair on her arm instantly stood on end, and she turned toward him.

"Don't be like that." The gentle expression in his eyes made her long to wrap her arms around him.

"I'm not being like anything," she replied.

"Come on, Natalie."

She loved the way her name sounded on his lips. So intimate, like they were the only two people on the beach. But it was also like torture to her.

"Just go. Wouldn't want them to see us talking." She didn't mean it. She didn't want him to go, but she was struggling to make sense of their new friendship, worried there was no place for her in his life, and her frustration had gotten the better of her.

He shook his head sadly and left her standing there watching him walk away.

When she turned back to her friends, they were both wearing amused grins on their faces. "What?"

"He's got it bad for you," Trinity replied.

"No doubt about it," Olivia added.

"No, you guys." She looked in Colton's direction again then back at them. "You think?"

Olivia and Trinity looked at each other and back at Natalie once more. "Yes!" they replied in unison.

Natalie watched Colton and the guys move farther down the beach away from them. She wanted to go after him, to walk along the beach with him, to talk and laugh like they had for the past two days. Instead, she was left to think about everything that had happened between them and the probability that nothing would ever happen again.

22
His Girlfriend

When the sun rose on their first morning in Virginia Beach, Natalie was already out running along the shoreline. Even though it was vacation, she still needed to keep up her routine of running and conditioning for gymnastics. She had to stay strong. Running was also the best way she knew to clear her head and help her focus on what was important.

Her legs felt heavy, her body sluggish, after an unrestful night. After waking around three o'clock in the morning, she'd spent an hour staring at the ceiling before she had crawled out of bed and sat on the balcony wrapped in a blanket, gazing up at the night sky, until the glow of sunrise had called her to the beach.

Her mind replayed every moment of the trip with Colton. It was starting to feel like a dream. Surreal. Part of her wished she could go back to Saturday morning and take a different route to the school or leave the house five minutes earlier just so she wouldn't have to feel this way.

But then she thought about the conversations she and Colton had, the way they had bonded over her mom and his brother, the laughter and teasing, the sights they had seen along the way ... the kisses. They had been places together, shared the journey. And it was the best time she had ever had.

She took deep, steady breaths and pushed herself to keep running. As she neared the resort on her return, she saw a figure running toward her with a build similar to Colton's and remembered that he also liked to run. Her heart, already thumping wildly, sped to a rapid pace as the person moved closer, then sputtered back to normal when she realized it wasn't him.

"Morning," the man said.

"Morning," she replied with half sadness and half relief.

She slowed to a brisk walk and caught her breath, stopping to sit on one of the beach chairs at their resort. She squeezed her shoulders and rubbed her neck, still stiff from the accident. Her attention turned to the sky, streaked in oranges and yellows—almost as yellow in some places as Colton's car. Why couldn't she get him out of her mind? Was this how it was going to be now? Every little thing reminding her of Colton?

She headed through the gate that led into the resort pool and on into the lobby. The elevator doors opened before her and out stepped Lexi with the Hannahs at her sides. They looked like triplets with their blonde hair pulled back in identical ponytails, all of them dressed in pink.

Natalie held in a breath and stood still while they exited, completely prepared for them to say something awful to her. Instead, they walked past without a word.

She entered the elevator and let out the breath, relieved when the doors finally moved to close.

A hand suddenly slipped into the gap, and the doors slid open again.

Lexi stood before her. "Do you want to come to breakfast with us?"

"Breakfast? With you?" Natalie couldn't believe her ears.

"Yeah. It's the least I can do."

Natalie shook her head. "You don't owe me anything, Lexi."

"I do. So, please, come."

She had an uneasy feeling about it, but her curiosity was piqued. Why was Lexi being so nice? Especially after all the mean messages during the trip. The only thing she could gather was that Colton had told her to stop. "Breakfast."

"See you at the restaurant in an hour?"

Natalie nodded hesitantly.

Lexi removed her hand from the door and gave a cutesy wave as the elevator door closed between them.

With the edge of a towel, Natalie swiped across the fogged mirror in the bathroom and stared at her reflection. Colton would be crazy to let go of a beautiful girl like Lexi for someone as simple and plain as her. She shook her head. She really had to stop thinking about him or she would ruin her entire vacation.

Natalie wandered from the bathroom. The sound of Trinity's subtle snoring filled the room. The three of them had stayed up late talking and catching up—mostly about Natalie and Colton's trip. Trinity had fallen asleep first, and Natalie and Olivia seriously considered digging through her bag and freezing all her bras like they had when they were young girls at slumber parties. Natalie vaguely remembered glancing at the clock with heavy eyelids around one o'clock as Olivia started to tell her something, but she couldn't remember what because she had drifted off.

She should've been more tired than Trinity and Olivia, considering she'd woken up in the middle of the night and hadn't gone back to sleep. But Natalie had never been one to sleep in. Occasionally, she would sleep until nine, but she'd been up early every day for most of her life and had developed an internal alarm clock.

When she was a baby, her father would put her in a stroller and take her along on his morning runs. As she had grown older and was training harder for gymnastics, she would run along with him, which soon became their morning tradition. Running alone on the beach earlier made her miss him and exacerbated her guilt over lying to him about the trip. A dark cloud hovered over her that she knew she couldn't avoid for long. She had to come clean, and it had to be soon, or it would eat away at her. It already was.

Once dressed, she combed through her hair and twisted it up into a messy bun atop her head before plopping down on the end of the queen bed Olivia and Trinity shared.

Olivia groaned.

Trinity slapped at the air, totally missing Natalie.

"Good morning, sleepyheads." Natalie's voice was light and chipper.

"Why?" Olivia mumbled. "Why can't you sleep in on vacation?"

"Because it's a beautiful day." Natalie yanked the covers off of her friends. "And I'm hungry. Who wants to go to breakfast with me ... and Lexi?"

"Pass." Trinity yanked the covers back over her head for a second, then flipped them down and sat up. "Wait, did you say Lexi?"

"I ran into her by the elevators, and she asked me to breakfast, but I really don't want to go alone."

"I'm there." She flipped the blankets back and her legs over the side of the bed. "But I'd rather sleep for another four hours."

Natalie rolled her eyes. "How about you, Liv? I need my girls with me."

Olivia squinted as she opened her eyes, focusing on Natalie's face then over at the clock on the nightstand. "Yeah, I could eat."

Natalie giggled and watched as Olivia sat up and stretched her arms above her head.

"I'm afraid this is some kind of prank Lexi's trying to pull on me or something." Natalie stood and walked over to the glass doors. "She's being way too nice to me since we got here."

"Yeah, you never know what's going through that evil mind of hers." Trinity let out a villainous laugh, which had them all giggling.

Downstairs at the breakfast buffet, there was no sign of Lexi and the Hannahs, so the girls found a seat off to the side by themselves.

"Do you think Colton told her to be nice to you?" Trinity asked as they scooped scrambled eggs and sausage onto their plates.

"That's what I was thinking," Olivia added.

"I don't know. He told me he was going to get her to stop with the cruel messages and those stopped. But I'm not sure him saying that would be enough to get her to make nice."

"Yeah, that seems odd." Olivia took a bite of her eggs.

"This is so confusing. I'm not sure if anything he told me was true or if he was just saying things he thought I wanted to hear."

"Why do you say that?" Trinity asked.

"He said he wanted to break up with her, but if he'd done it, there's no way she wouldn't be out to get me right now."

"Oh, I'm sure he was being sincere." Olivia gave her a reassuring smile.

Natalie managed a weak smile in return. "I'd like to think that the Colton I got to know on our road trip is the real Colton. I really would. Everything just feels different now, and I don't even know how to act around him."

"Just be you," Olivia said. "You're who he got to know, so don't be any different than you were on the trip."

"It's just not the same. I can't be with him when he's with his friends. And there's no time when I can really talk to him this week. It'll have to be up to him, I guess, because there's no way I'm pulling him away from his friends without knowing if he really wants to talk to me. It would be embarrassing if he blew me off in front of them."

"True," Olivia replied. "But I don't think he would blow you off. Not after the way he was looking at you last night.

"I was *just* gonna say the same thing," Trinity said. "He wants you in his life. I can tell there's more there."

"Don't lose hope," Olivia added.

Natalie let out a deep breath and took a bite of her eggs.

"Did you ever imagine you would end up in a car with Colton for two days?" Trinity asked.

She shook her head. "It still sort of feels like it didn't happen, which is probably why I'm so confused about the whole thing."

"It'll work out." Trinity chewed her sausage. "I know it will."

"Me too. And we're on your side," Olivia assured her. "Always."

"I know." Natalie knew how lucky she was to have such devoted friends. She scanned the room as she finished off the last bites of her breakfast. Still no sign of Lexi and her friends. She wondered if that had been Lexi's plan all along—to lure her to breakfast alone and then stand her up.

"So much for Lexi being nice to me."

Trinity and Olivia rolled their eyes in reply.

After a perfect day of walking along the boardwalk, shopping for souvenirs, and taking pictures by the statue of Neptune at the park, the girls returned to the resort in the late afternoon to spend a little time at the pool before dinner.

Natalie slathered on the sunscreen, already feeling that her cheeks and shoulders were a little warm from all their walking in the sun that day. She spread her towel over one of the lounge chairs and settled onto it, leaning back to relax.

"Cannonball!" someone shouted as they jumped into the pool, sending a large wave her way.

Natalie screamed as the cool water doused her from head to toe.

Olivia and Trinity, who were standing far enough back not to be affected by more than a few sprinkles, cracked up at their wet friend.

Natalie wiped her eyes and looked at the culprit.

"You look even hotter wet." Grant gave her a flirty grin and swam away.

She narrowed her eyes at him.

Lexi stood across the pool watching the scene, wearing a skimpy bikini and a not-so-friendly expression.

"Sorry about him." Colton was suddenly standing over her.

Her pulse quickened.

"I have to agree with him, though." He winked and jumped into the pool behind his cocky friend.

Natalie held in a smile and lay back with eyes closed to let the sun dry her.

Trinity and Olivia settled in next to Natalie and kept chattering about this or that, but Natalie wasn't really listening. Just knowing Colton was nearby was enough to distract her from everything else.

Natalie peeked toward the pool. Colton was playing a game of chicken with Grant, Lexi, and one of the Hannahs. He seemed to glow in the light of the sun—golden highlights in his honey-brown hair, skin tanned from a day in the sun, green eyes sparkling as they caught the reflection off the surface of the pool. She forced her eyes closed again and savored the warmth of the sun against her face, trying her best to tune out their laughter. Her thoughts returned to the little green tent on the mountaintop, lying in Colton's arms, his fingertips running through her hair, his hand caressing her back. Then they were in the car, his hands holding her face, his lips ...

"Sorry about breakfast."

Natalie jerked awake and cracked her eyelids to see Lexi standing over her. How long had she been asleep? She peeked across the pool and saw Colton sitting on the edge with his legs dangling in the water, laughing at something one of the guys had said. She squinted up at Lexi, but what she really wanted was to sink back into her dream as quickly as possible.

"I meant to meet you, but Colton wanted to go for a bike ride, and we ended up picking up some food and having a breakfast picnic together. It was so romantic."

She felt sick to the stomach. "No worries. I ate with my friends."

"Tomorrow instead?" Lexi asked.

"Tomorrow's the trip to Jamestown. Sorry."

"We'll do lunch another day then." Lexi walked around the pool toward Colton without waiting for Natalie's reply.

Natalie wasn't going to hold her breath, and she honestly didn't care whether they had a meal together or not. In fact, she sort of hoped it didn't work out. Something still felt off about how nice Lexi was being. Why the sudden need to be BFFs?

"Why do you give her the time of day?" Trinity asked when Lexi was out of earshot.

Natalie shrugged. "Keep your enemies closer, right?"

Trinity laughed. "Truth."

"Hey, there's something I've been wanting to talk to you about," Olivia said.

Natalie peeked across the pool at Colton and his friends again. He and Lexi were now floating near the corner of the pool, her arms and legs wrapped around him. A knot formed in her stomach as she watched them. Whatever Colton had said made Lexi throw her head back and laugh loud enough for everyone to hear.

She couldn't take it anymore. "I'm sorry. I've gotta get out of here." She scrambled from her seat, gathered her things as quickly as possible, and headed to their room.

Trinity and Olivia came not long after.

"Are you OK?" Trinity asked. "It must be hard for you to see them together."

"Let's get cleaned up and go to dinner. You'll feel better after you eat," Olivia assured her.

"I'm not hungry." She threw on her running clothes rather than showering. "I need a run."

"Natty, come with us," Olivia begged.

"I'm sorry, Liv, I just have to clear my head."

Natalie ran down the beach for the second time that day, earbuds in, listening to Taylor Swift. She ran full speed until she couldn't run anymore, then kept walking until she was a good four miles from the resort. Walking back gave her plenty of time to think.

She couldn't pinpoint one emotion—sadness, guilt, hurt, embarrassment. It was her own fault for making the stupid decision to take the alternate route away from the hotel pitstop in West Virginia, for sleeping in the tent with Colton, for letting herself get close to him—emotionally *and* physically. And for what? He seemed no closer to ending his relationship with Lexi. He'd given her no guarantee that he ever would. He'd made her no promises.

If she didn't put the road trip behind her, she would be miserable for the rest of her vacation. So she resolved to do just that and to steer clear of Colton and Lexi. She couldn't let them ruin this week she had been looking forward to all year.

When she returned to the room, the girls were gone. Exhausted from lack of sleep, head pounding, neck still aching from her whiplash, she took a quick shower, threw on her pajamas, and fell asleep before her head hit the pillow.

23
History

Trinity grumbled as she and Olivia took their seats on the bus across the aisle from Natalie.

"Come on, you guys. It'll be fun," Natalie assured them.

"So you say," Trinity replied. "The cozy bed is calling me back."

"You can sleep in at home any time you want. How often do we get to see places that have to do with the history of our country?"

Trinity shook her head. "You're way too excited about history."

"I like seeing new places. Don't you?"

"I was fine seeing the boardwalk and the beach."

Natalie smiled. "Thanks for coming with me."

Trinity gave her a thumbs-up, but Olivia remained quiet. She had been quiet all morning, in fact.

"Everything OK, Liv?" Natalie asked.

"Fine," Olivia replied.

Uh-oh. She knew her best friend, and that was not an honest *fine*. But before she had a chance to question her again, she was startled by a hand on her shoulder.

"Is this seat taken?"

Her gaze lifted, and her heart skipped a beat at Colton standing there before her. "You're not signed up for this," she blurted.

He smiled at her. "I am now. Can I sit?"

"Sure." Her stomach fluttered, and she scooted over to the seat closest to the window. "Wouldn't you have more fun playing chicken in the pool with your friends?"

He plopped down in the seat next to her, his thigh pressed against hers, and patted her knee. "You can't get rid of me, Nat. I told you I wanted to hang out with you this week."

"I thought you were just saying that. I didn't think you actually meant it."

"Why not?"

"Because." She stared out the window at the parking lot.

"That's not an answer." He leaned forward, angling into her until she looked at him.

She was flustered being so close to him again. "Because the bubble has popped. Back to reality. Back where we belong."

"Are we? Really? Because this is the first time since we got here that I feel like I'm exactly where I'm supposed to be."

When he said things like that, she wanted to believe him. She wanted it to be true. Because she agreed. Sitting next to him felt right, like they were supposed to be there. Together. Like everything that had happened on their trip wasn't just some crazy fluke.

Despite her earlier resolve, she touched his hand, and the biggest smile spread across his face.

"Hi, Colton." Trinity interrupted their moment.

He looked across the aisle.

"You know Trinity and Olivia," Natalie said.

"Hey," he greeted them. "Are you girls having fun so far?"

"On this bus? Not so much," Trinity replied.

Colton chuckled.

"Thanks for bringing Natalie down here. It wouldn't have been the same without her."

"That's for sure," Colton replied.

Still Olivia said nothing.

Colton turned his attention back to Natalie, his eyes traveling over her face. He tapped her nose with his index finger. "Got a little sun yesterday, did ya?"

"A little." She wiggled her nose, which was not quite as red as Rudolph the Red-Nosed Reindeer, but close. "I should've put extra sunscreen on my nose, I guess."

He leaned into her shoulder and his mouth curved up to the right. "You look cute."

The scent of coconut sunscreen and mint mouthwash invaded her nostrils. She shoved aside the sudden longing for minty kisses and rolled her eyes. "Sure."

"You really need to learn to take a compliment."

"What, like Grant's comment yesterday?"

"He's not subtle."

She feigned shock. "You don't say?"

Colton smiled.

"Doesn't it bother you? The way he talks to girls?"

"I mean, he can be rude sometimes, but what can I say? He's a flirt. It's just who he is."

Natalie rolled her eyes again.

Colton looked at her seriously. "And he's my friend."

"I know he is."

"Don't you have any friends who do things you hate?"

Natalie thought for a moment. "Not really." Unless she counted Lexi.

"Well, you're lucky."

She was well aware of that fact. After her friendship with Lexi fell apart, it was easy to see who her true friends were, and it made her appreciate them even more.

"Speaking of friends, you couldn't drag yours along today?"

Colton laughed. It *was* pretty ridiculous to think that anyone in his crowd would attend an educational day trip instead of hanging out at the beach. Lexi wouldn't be caught dead on a trip like this.

"Hey, did you say something to Lexi about me?" She was curious about Lexi's overly friendly behavior.

Colton shook his head. "Not really. Why?"

"Well, if you told her to stop harassing me, thank you. She's been ... better."

"I did mention it to her again, but I didn't think she was listening," he said with a smirk.

Maybe that explained Lexi's change of heart toward her.

"I also asked her why you two aren't friends anymore."

Her eyes widened. "What did she say?" Natalie was anxious for the answer, because she truly wished she knew what had changed between them.

"She said it was ancient history, back when you were in elementary school."

That wasn't the answer she was hoping for. "It wasn't elementary school." She shook her head. "Whatever. It doesn't matter now."

"I won't let her bother you."

"I'm not sure there's much you can do if she decides to come after me again."

He raised an eyebrow. "Trust me, there is."

"Anyway, thanks for standing up for me."

He leaned his shoulder against hers. "I always will."

She wanted to believe that, more than anything, but so far, it seemed he only meant it when it was convenient for him.

The bus pulled into the parking lot of the Jamestown Settlement and let the students off at the door. They entered and made their way through the displays in the historical gallery. Natalie was fascinated by all the artifacts and the replicas of settlers' homes. History was one of her passions and something she had seriously considered studying when she got to college—maybe as a minor.

As they exited the main building, Natalie glanced over at Colton and found him watching her.

"What?"

"You like all this stuff, don't you?" he asked.

She nodded. "I really do."

"Well, I have to admit, it's not as boring as ..." His words trailed off as he caught sight of three ships docked just past the replica of the fort that once stood at Jamestown. "I want to see the ships."

She laughed at the look of boyish excitement on his face.

They walked to the fort first and wandered through the buildings—the blacksmith, the living quarters, the armory. The sound of a rifle firing came from the nearby stage, where a man dressed in settler's garb was demonstrating how to load and fire a black powder rifle.

Colton suddenly took Natalie's hand and led her through the doors of the church. They sat together on one of the heavy wooden pews toward the back and listened to a woman in historical clothing talk about the building and the history.

Natalie's eyes scanned the room from the raised pulpit to the candlesticks attached to the rafters to The Ten Commandments and The Lord's Prayer written in old style calligraphy that graced the walls. She tried to imagine the settlers in a church like this, her thoughts returning to the little service they had attended at the campground, the worshipful choruses echoing in her mind.

When the tour was over, the woman walked to the back and unwound a rope tied near the door. She asked for a volunteer and chose a young boy to help her ring the church bells. The boy laughed as the rope pulled his arm a little and the bells sounded.

Colton looked over at Natalie and smiled. They exited the building with his hand on her lower back. "Can we go see the ships now?"

She cracked up as he rushed ahead of her to the fort exit.

"This is what I'm talking about." Colton pulled out his phone and took some pictures of the ships—re-creations of the *Susan Constant*, *Godspeed*, and *Discovery*, which brought the English colonists to Virginia in 1607. He grabbed Natalie's arm and tucked her into his side, holding his phone out for a selfie.

"Are you gonna post that?" she asked.

"Not if you don't want me to."

"I'd rather you didn't." She didn't need to give Lexi any more ammunition. "But send it to me."

A few taps on his screen and her phone dinged.

She opened the picture. "Nice."

"Come on!" He grabbed her arm and dragged her along behind him and up the gangplank of the *Discovery*, obviously excited to board the ship.

She nearly dropped her phone because of him. Again.

They walked around the deck first, then made their way down into the belly of the ship. The interior of the boat was cramped, and she couldn't imagine the settlers making the long journey across the ocean from England in such tight quarters.

When they came to the sleeping chambers, Natalie leaned into Colton's back and peeked over his shoulder to get a better view. "That's crazy small."

"We could fit."

She smacked him on the back and moved away.

"We fit in that sleeping bag together," he said.

Her gaze traveled back over her shoulder, and she was about to remind him that it was a two-person sleeping bag when she noticed the flirtatious look in his eyes.

"We could make *this* work." He nodded enthusiastically.

"Oh my gosh." She walked away, shaking her head, the warmth of his presence close behind.

Natalie climbed the stairs to the upper deck and walked out to the bow. Colton moved to stand behind her and grabbed her wrists, lifting her arms up until they were straight out to each side.

"Are you flying?" he whispered.

"Colton!" She yanked her arms from his grip. "We are *not* recreating the scene from *Titanic*."

He busted up laughing, which turned into a groan when she elbowed him in the gut.

When they exited the ship, Natalie saw Olivia and Trinity standing not too far away next to the *Godspeed*. She ran over to catch up with them while Colton boarded the *Susan Constant*.

Olivia's eyes met hers. "Are you two having fun?" Her voice held more than a hint of annoyance.

Natalie nodded. "We are. Colton is like a kid on these ships."

Olivia rolled her eyes.

"What's wrong, Liv?"

Natalie looked at Trinity, who stood quietly to the side, then back at Olivia.

"I thought we were going to see this together, and then you two took off."

"Oh, we didn't mean to. We lost track of you in the museum," Natalie explained.

"You have a phone. You could've texted me or waited for us." Olivia's tone had become harsh.

"I'm sorry, Liv. I didn't think this was such a big deal to you. You guys didn't even want to come."

Olivia's eyes fixed on hers again. "You're right. I wish I hadn't."

"I'm glad you came. I am." Natalie felt awful, and she desperately wanted to make it up to her best friend. "Wanna go check out the Native American village together?"

"Fine." Olivia rotated on her heel and started walking in the other direction.

Natalie spotted Colton walking along the deck of the ship. She took her phone from her back pocket and fired off a quick text letting him know where she was going. It was a very couple-y thing to do. And they weren't a couple. But it felt natural—almost second nature—to let him know.

Her phone chimed with his text.

Cole:
I'm almost done being Cap'n Jack.
See ya over there.

She smiled as she slid the phone into her back pocket again.

"You really like him, don't you?" Trinity was grinning at her as they walked along behind Olivia.

"I can't help it. When we're together, it's so fun and natural. And when we're not, all I can think about is being close to him again."

"And kissing him. In the car. In the middle of a thunderstorm." Trinity practically swooned.

Natalie could almost still feel his lips on hers and a warmth spread through her body that had nothing to do with the sticky temperature outside.

The girls walked into one of the re-created Powhatan domed dwellings. It was more spacious than it appeared from the outside, with plenty of room to move and sleep. There was even a fire circle in the center with a vent atop the dome to release the smoke. Animal hides were everywhere—displayed along the thatched walls, strewn about on cots, stretched outside on a rack to dry. Fishing nets, handmade baskets, and quivers full of arrows hung near the door.

Natalie turned too quickly to exit and bumped into Olivia, nearly knocking her over. "Sorry, Liv."

"Watch what you're doing," Olivia snapped.

"What is wrong with you?" Natalie snapped back. "I apologized for losing you earlier, but I know it's not that. You've been acting weird all day."

"Don't worry yourself about it. You'll find out soon enough."

"What does that mean?"

Olivia pushed past her and ducked through the door.

Natalie's mouth dropped open, and she looked at Trinity. "What is going on?"

"I can't say."

She tilted her head. "You can't or you won't."

"She told me not to tell you. She wants to be the one."

"Tell me what?"

Trinity pressed her lips together. "Sorry. Talk to Liv."

"How can I if she won't talk to me?"

Trinity shrugged.

Natalie blew out an exasperated breath and left the hut. Colton was just walking up, but Natalie looked past him in search of Olivia, who was nearing the main building again.

"Hungry?" Colton asked. "Because I'm starved."

Natalie simply nodded, and the three of them walked along the path to the main building. Colton and Trinity chatted about the ships as they moved down the hallway to the main lobby and entered the restaurant, but all she could think about was the look on Olivia's face as she had walked out.

Olivia was already through the line at the restaurant and seated at a table by herself when they arrived.

"I'm going to sit with her," Trinity informed them. "Maybe you should give her some space."

It broke Natalie's heart that Olivia was upset with her. She wished she knew why. And the last thing in the world she wanted was to give her space. She wanted to fix whatever was wrong and get back to normal.

"What's that all about?" Colton asked.

"I don't know." Her eyes burned with tears.

"Hey." Colton put his arm around her and squeezed. "Don't cry."

She wiped away an escaped tear and placed a chicken salad sandwich and chips on her tray.

"Did you girls fight?"

Natalie shook her head. "I don't know why she's mad at me."

"I'm sure you'll work it out."

"I hope you're right."

Natalie hadn't planned to fall asleep, but she *had* been weary from the long day of walking around in the heat and wiped out emotionally. When the bus hit a bump, she jerked awake and discovered herself tucked against Colton's chest. She could hear his heart beating under her cheek, feel the rise and fall of his chest as he breathed and the warmth of his arm wrapped around her shoulders. She lifted her head to find his eyes closed, a contented smile on his face.

Across the aisle, Trinity was giving them a goofy grin and a thumbs-up, but Olivia was in a world of her own, her head leaning against the window as she stared out at the passing landscape.

Natalie hadn't expected Olivia's reaction to Colton spending the day with them. In fact, she had expected the opposite, since Olivia had been the one teasing about the two of them and telling her it would all work out. But Olivia seemed to have changed her tune, and Natalie didn't understand why.

And what did she mean when she said "You'll find out soon enough"? What was Olivia not telling her?

Colton shifted, and she sat up. He opened his eyes and frowned at her. "You didn't have to move."

"I didn't mean to fall asleep on you," she said.

"I like sleeping with you."

She blushed a little.

"Not like we haven't done it before." His sly grin deepened the shade of pink in her cheeks.

Natalie peered out the window, anxious to change the subject, and noticed they were traveling on the Hampton Bay Bridge, as they had on the day of their arrival. "There's the underwater tunnel up ahead." She couldn't bring herself to look at him again. "Still scared?"

"I wasn't scared," he answered defensively.

"Whatevs."

The bus entered the tunnel, and Colton leaned close to her ear. "Will you meet me tonight?"

She angled her head toward him, nearly touching her ear to his lips. "Where?"

"The Ferris wheel at nine."

"Why?" Her eyelids slid closed at the feel of his breath on her neck.

"Just meet me."

Natalie swallowed hard. "It's probably not a good idea."

"It's the best idea I've had all day." His whispered words sent goosebumps racing across her skin.

She turned her head, their lips millimeters from touching.

"Say yes." His gaze fell to her lips.

She couldn't deny him anything when they were close like this. "Yes."

The blare of sunlight as they exited the tunnel brought them back to reality. Colton straightened and sat back with a look of satisfaction.

"Can I walk you back?" Colton asked.

"You don't have to do that."

"I want to." His fingertips traced along the inside of her forearm, across her wrist, and into her palm.

He's going to hold my hand. Right now. In public.

But as quickly as the thought came, he moved his hand away.

Grant and a couple friends walked toward them as they headed for the elevators. "Awww, look guys, it's Nat King Cole."

"What's that?" Colton seemed only mildly annoyed.

"That's your couple name. Get it? Nat ..." He pointed at Natalie. "King Cole." He pointed at Colton. "Like that singer from the olden days."

Natalie was not amused. She wanted so badly to tell him to stop calling Colton that.

Colton rolled his eyes and led her past them.

"Hey!" Grant called after them. "Where have you two been all day?"

"Jamestown," Colton answered matter-of-factly.

Grant and the guys laughed. "You went on that field trip? Oh, now I know something's seriously wrong with you."

"Why do you have to be like that?" Colton stopped and turned toward his friend.

"Like what?"

"I don't have to spend every day with you guys. What's the big deal?"

"It's nothing to me." Grant touched his hands to his chest. "But it's a pretty big deal to your girlfriend."

"That's none of your business, G."

"It is when she makes it my business."

Colton's eyes narrowed. "What does that mean?"

"It means she keeps crying to me about it. If you don't want her, cut her loose, man. You're not doing anyone any favors by lying."

Colton took a step toward Grant. "I didn't lie to her. I told her exactly where I was going today."

"Whatever you say." He motioned for the other guys to follow him. "Grant, come on."

Grant waved Colton off as they walked on through the lobby.

Colton groaned and pressed the elevator button.

"I knew it was going to be like this," Natalie said.

He turned to face her.

She motioned back and forth between the two of them. "*This* is messing up all your friendships and making everything weird." Not that she was fond of Grant or any of Colton's friends for that matter, but she didn't want to be the one to cause the end of a lifelong friendship either.

"I don't care about any of that," he said seriously.

"You and Grant have been friends since you were kids. I don't want to cause trouble there. You should go talk to him."

"Our friendship has been changing a lot this year. It isn't the same as it used to be. And once we graduate, things are going to change even more. We're going different directions in life. There's no getting around it. It's inevitable." He stared off down the hallway even though Grant and their buddies were long gone.

She chewed on her bottom lip, feeling guilty for causing a rift in their friendship.

"I'm just glad *we're* friends." He put his arm around her as the elevator door opened.

She smiled up at him. "Me too."

Colton took a step toward the elevator, but she stopped and spun out from under his arm.

"You don't have to walk me to my room. Really, it's fine."

"I told you I would," he replied.

"I'll just see you tonight, OK?"

He pursed his lips and nodded. "Nine o'clock."

"I'll be there." The elevator doors closed between them, and Natalie sighed. Part of her was afraid that if he came up to her room, she might be tempted to let him kiss her again, and that could never happen as long as he was still with Lexi.

The smell of popcorn wafted through the air as Natalie entered the little amusement park a block from the boardwalk. All evening, she had been going over and over the conversation she needed to have with Colton. But she was afraid that when the time came, she wouldn't be able to put her thoughts into the words she had so carefully considered.

An uneasiness had settled in her stomach too over whatever was bothering Olivia. She had said no more than two words to Natalie all evening, despite Natalie pressing her to talk. They had fought lots of times over the years, but always over silly things. This felt bigger, and she wished Olivia would just tell her what it was already.

When Natalie spotted Colton standing next to the Ferris wheel, tickets in hand, aquamarine shirt making the color of his eyes pop, she almost turned around and headed back to the resort. Because all of the things she wanted to say to him flew straight out of her mind in that moment.

"Natalie!" he called.

Too late to run away now.

His expression softened as she approached, his eyes giving her a once over. He tapped the expensive watch on his wrist. "I was starting to think you stood me up."

"Almost did," she admitted. She couldn't help it. He brought out the honesty in her.

"Well, I'm glad you're here." He took her hand in his, leading her into the line for the Ferris wheel. "You look really pretty tonight."

Trinity had let her borrow a pair of khaki shorts and a teal blouse with a double ruffle across the top that only covered one of her shoulders. Looking at the two of them, one might think they dressed to match on purpose, like those cheesy couples she had sometimes seen and secretly wished she were a part of.

"Thanks. You too." She shook her head. "You look nice, I mean."

He smiled as they stepped up and took their place on the Ferris wheel. The operator moved the wheel around, raising them a little higher with each new set of riders.

"There's something I've been wanting to say to you," Natalie began.

"I have something I want to say too."

"Go ahead." She was relieved, too nervous at this point to say what she came to say anyway.

"You know I like you and—"

"Colton."

He squeezed her hand and continued. "No matter what happens the rest of this week, I want there to be an *us* when the week is over."

As the wheel lifted them again, Natalie took in a deep breath and let it out. She couldn't believe what she was hearing. It was what she had imagined and fantasized about in a million different scenarios over the years. But it wasn't right. He shouldn't be saying things like that when he still had a girlfriend.

Her stomach dropped as the Ferris wheel began moving around more rapidly. "So, my parents had this huge fight during a really bad storm once." It wasn't what she had planned to say first, but it came blurting out.

"One of your bad memories?" There was sincere concern in his eyes.

She nodded. "The reason they were fighting was because my dad found out my mom had slept with another man."

His jaw dropped. "Whoa, seriously?"

155

"Yeah." She scrunched up her nose, hating that she had to talk about it. "He was someone my dad considered a friend. And once the truth came out, that friendship was ruined. It was really hard for him."

"That sucks."

She nodded. "I've seen firsthand what cheating can do to a person—"

He held up his hand. "I know where you're going with this, but Lexi and I have been falling apart for a while now."

Natalie let out an exasperated puff of air. "But you haven't broken up with her, have you?"

The shake of his head was so subtle, she almost missed it.

"Right, so, you're still together. And you kissed me. And you keep pursuing me. All while you have a girlfriend."

"I know." He looked down, ashamed.

"Lexi doesn't deserve to be cheated on. No girl does. If you aren't getting along anymore, you should be man enough to tell her it's over before you kiss another girl. And I don't want to be the other girl in this scenario. Especially after seeing what my dad went through. It's kind of a deal breaker for me. "

He rubbed his fingertips back and forth across his brow. "I'm really sorry. You deserve better than that."

"So does Lexi."

"I know that." He shook his head. "This is not how I saw tonight going."

"I just needed you to know how I feel."

He shifted in his seat to look at her. "I'm going to make it right, OK? It's just ... it's complicated. We've been together on-and-off for the past four years."

"You do what you need to do." She hoped he would, because there was no chance for them if he didn't.

He lifted his hand and cupped her cheek.

Her stomach flipped at his touch. As much as she wanted another kiss, she wanted to be sure she was the only one he was kissing.

"I promise not to kiss you again," he told her.

Her mouth fell open a little. Not what she was hoping to hear.

His lips curved up to the right, showing off the dimple. "Until I'm free to."

24
Secrets and Fears

The sun was hiding behind the clouds and the air was cooler than the rest of the week had been. It was like the weather knew how Natalie was feeling and decided to match her mood.

The day was made for shopping, and it was clear by the foot traffic in the shops that every other vacationer had the exact same thing in mind. Cloudy and cold meant emptying funds from wallets.

The entire day felt off, especially shopping with Olivia, who kept her distance from Natalie and Trinity, browsing racks on the opposite side of stores, walking so that Trinity was between them, only speaking when spoken to. Natalie never would've imagined a day with her best friends could be so awkward.

On top of that, she hadn't seen Colton all day, which saddened her. They hadn't spoken much after their Ferris wheel conversation. It had been a quiet, slightly uncomfortable walk back to the resort, and it left her unsure of where they stood. Were they still friends? Did he really understand?

A part of her wished she had kept her mouth shut about her mom cheating, because things had been going so well up until then. But deep inside, she knew it was how she truly felt. As much as she had grown to care for him, she knew it was the right thing to say and hoped he would take it to heart.

As the girls browsed the racks of clothing, Natalie found herself wondering where Colton was and what he was doing. At lunch, she wondered if he had made things right with Grant. And when the end of the day neared and they headed to the amusement park, she wondered if he would be there again. With Lexi. Or if he had finally told her how he felt.

The answer to that last question made itself known when Natalie left the amusement park restroom and rounded the corner past one of the concession stands to find Lexi and Grant off by themselves in what appeared to be a heated conversation. Natalie stepped back and moved around the other side, staying out of sight, hoping to hear what they were fighting about.

"We can't keep doing this." Lexi pushed Grant's hand away from her arm. "If Colton knew about us, he would never forgive me. Or you."

"You think I haven't thought about that?" Grant ran his fingers through his hair. "He's my best friend."

"Exactly, which is why we have to stop."

Grant took Lexi's face in his hands and gazed into her eyes. "I can't stop thinking about you. I don't want this to end. Don't throw away what we have. We're too good together, baby."

"Grant." Lexi lowered her head as she grabbed hold of his forearms.

"These past six months have turned my world upside down." He moved closer.

"Please don't."

"Screw Colton. He doesn't appreciate what he has."

Lexi looked into his eyes then.

"But I do. I know what I've got, and I would never take you for granted, like he has." He leaned forward then and pressed his lips to hers.

She didn't fight him off. Quite the opposite, in fact. They were all over each other. So much that Natalie averted her eyes then left as quickly as she could.

Now what? She had no idea what to do with this new information. *They've been going behind Colton's back for six months?* Should she tell Colton? If she did, that would be the end of him and Lexi, she knew that for sure. But should she really be the one to tell him? *No! Lexi and Grant should tell him.* But how could she make that happen?

Natalie was on her way to rejoin Olivia and Trinity, when she suddenly turned on her heel and marched back to the cheating couple.

"Hey!" Her single word startled them apart.

Lexi looked panicked and swung her arm at Grant, slapping him across the cheek. "How dare you."

He held his cheek. "What was that for?"

"For kissing me."

Natalie shook her head in disgust. "Nice try. I heard your conversation before. I know what's going on."

Lexi glared at her. "You have no idea. And it's none of your business anyway."

"Colton and I are friends and—"

"Since when?" Lexi snapped.

"Since our trip down here, and no matter what you think, he cares about you. Both of you. And if you care about him, you will tell him what's been going on."

"Stay away from Colton," Lexi demanded.

"You obviously have no respect for him or your relationship, so why do you care if I'm friends with him?"

"We've been together for a long time." Lexi put her hand on her hip. "You don't know anything about him after two days together in a car."

"I know a lot more about him than you think I do."

Lexi glared at her. "I doubt that."

"None of that matters. What does is the fact that you betrayed him." Natalie looked at Grant then. "You two have been best friends since you were kids. Is she really worth risking that?"

"Screw you!" Lexi cried.

"We're not just fooling around," Grant replied. "I'm in love with her."

"What?" Lexi's head whipped in Grant's direction.

"I love you, Lex," he declared sincerely.

Tears filled Lexi's eyes. "Are you kidding me? You love me? I told you I didn't want anything serious."

"I can't help it that things changed for me." Grant wrapped his fingers around her wrist.

Lexi looked visibly shaken.

"You need to decide what you want, Lexi," Natalie said.

"Get out of here, Natalie!"

It was the first time Lexi had addressed her by her name since the seventh grade.

"We used to be friends," Natalie reminded her.

Lexi stared off at nothing in particular.

"And no matter what you've done to me over the years, I still care about you and the friendship we used to have."

"I said get out of here!" Lexi's eyes shot to Natalie's, and she pointed toward the exit. "Go!"

Natalie shook her head and left her former best friend and the guy she was cheating with behind. She marched away, disgusted and confused. If ever there was a solution to her situation with Colton, this was it.

Olivia and Trinity met up with her, curious expressions on their faces from witnessing the end of the conversation.

"What was that all about?" Trinity asked.

"I caught them kissing," Natalie revealed.

The girls' eyes widened.

"Are you serious?" Olivia stared across the park at them.

"Well, that's good news, isn't it?" Trinity asked as Natalie grabbed their arms and turned them away from Lexi and Grant.

"I'm not telling Colton," Natalie stated before either girl had a chance to say it.

Trinity's mouth fell open. "Why not?"

"Because *they* have to be the ones to tell him. I won't be the one to ruin their relationships."

"But he deserves to know," Trinity stated.

"He does. But he won't find out from me."

Olivia didn't say anything. She simply walked along with the two of them until they were out of range of the couple.

"If I were you, I'd be jumping for joy and running as fast as I could to find him," Trinity said, "because this will be the end of them and the start of something for you guys."

Natalie shrugged her shoulders. "Maybe. But maybe not."

Trinity looked at her curiously. "Why do you say that?"

"He's going to school at MSU. I'm going to Arizona. I'm not sure a new relationship could withstand that much distance. He'll probably meet some beautiful, brilliant girl at school and fall in love. And maybe I'll meet somebody down there. I don't know."

"If he came to you right now and told you that he and Lexi were over and he wanted to be with you, you wouldn't jump at the chance?"

"I don't know."

Trinity waved her off. "You're just scared. You've never had a real long-term relationship before, and you're afraid to try."

"That's not it."

"Yes, it is." Olivia finally piped in. "You've been in love with Colton Daynes since you were six years old, and now you finally have a chance to be with him and that terrifies you." Her tone was bitter and snippy.

Natalie's mouth fell open.

"You're afraid to take the chance because of all the hurt you've faced in your past. But you'll be sorry. You'll regret not going for it."

"Why do you sound so mad at me?" Olivia had never spoken so harshly to her before.

"Because you have *everything* going for you—your scholarship, gymnastics, an amazing dad—and you're *so* close to getting the guy you like, but you're about to screw it all up."

"It's *my* life, Olivia."

"And you're afraid to live it." Olivia walked away in a huff.

Natalie stared after her blank-faced.

Olivia suddenly spun around and took two steps back. "I really thought this vacation was going to be about the three of us. Our last hurrah before graduation, remember? I thought maybe we'd get a chance to sit down and talk and I could tell you how I've been feeling and share my exciting news with you, but it's been all about Colton since we got here."

"That's not true. I've been with you and Trinity pretty much the entire time." Where was this coming from?

"But you haven't really been with us. Ever since you got here, you've been distracted."

"I can't explain it, Liv. I feel like I'm at a crossroads, at a transition. Things are about to change in so many huge ways."

"We're all at a crossroads, Natalie. Everything isn't always about you."

Natalie didn't know what to say.

"You should tell him." Olivia stared at her.

"I already told you, I'm not doing that." Natalie looked over at Trinity, as if seeking help, but she simply pressed her lips together.

"You never listen to me, Natalie," Olivia continued. "Whenever I give you advice, you ignore it. Even when it's the best advice anyone could've ever given you in your life."

"What're you talking about?"

Olivia turned and walked toward the exit. "I'm so tired of being dismissed."

Natalie rushed after her. "I don't dismiss you."

She spun around again. "Yes, you do. Every other person in your life gets higher priority than me, and I'm tired of it."

"Liv."

"Why can't you tell him?"

"I like him too much. I don't want to hurt him. I'll never forget the look on my dad's face when he found out my mom cheated, and I don't want to put that look on Colton's face." Natalie glanced over at the Ferris wheel. "Getting to know him on this trip, the conversations we had ... I felt so close to him. But it scared me too."

Olivia listened.

"I don't want to get hurt like my dad was. Maybe that whole experience scared me off of relationships."

"That's just stupid," Olivia blurted.

"Liv," Trinity scolded her.

"I'm sorry, but you can't hide from relationships because of that. They were married, and there was a whole lot more to their situation, a lot to do with your mom's health. Even your dad found love again after all that."

"What if I'm like her?" Natalie finally asked the question that had been hiding inside, unspoken for a very long time.

The girls stared blankly at her.

"What if I'm like my mom?" It terrified her to say the words aloud.

Olivia's eyes softened. "You're not your mom, Natalie."

Tears began to sting Natalie's eyes. "But what if I am? Sometimes I feel withdrawn and sad and alone. What if that's the beginnings of what my mom went through?"

"Your mother has a serious medical condition."

"I know. But some days I worry that I'll end up like her and hurt the ones I love." Natalie's eyes filled with tears.

"Your mom had already been hospitalized by the time she was your age, right?" Olivia asked. "You said she had suicidal tendencies by the time she was twelve. Is that how you feel? Suicidal?"

Natalie shook her head.

Olivia took Natalie's hand, the first kind gesture from her in days. "You're fine, Natalie. You're nothing like your mom. Don't let fear keep you from living. Don't let it stop you from falling in love."

Tears were streaming down Natalie's cheeks by then, and her friends wrapped their arms around her and held her while she cried.

As they were letting go, Grant walked by them in a huff, followed by Lexi, who was wiping away tears of her own.

"You ruin everything, you know that, Natalie Rhodes." Lexi gave her the evil eye and walked on.

"You're just jealous," Trinity called after her.

That stopped Lexi in her tracks, and she whipped around to face them. "That's a good one."

"It's the truth," Trinity said. "You can't stand the fact that Natalie succeeded in gymnastics when you didn't."

"That's ridiculous. I hate gymnastics, that's why I quit." The right side of Lexi's upper lip lifted in a snarl.

"Well, you used to love it when we were all on the team together."

"We were twelve," Lexi snapped.

"And you sucked at it."

"Trin," Natalie spoke softly to her friend, who could be a little too blunt at times.

"And now you hate that Natalie has the gymnastics scholarship you wanted." Trinity kept going. "And you hate that Colton cares more about her than he does about you."

"Trinity, that's enough," Natalie warned.

Lexi was shaking from anger. "I hate you. I hate you all." She fled the scene.

Natalie watched Lexi race for the exit and disappear down the street. She turned to Trinity. "You didn't have to do that to her."

"It was all the truth. You know it was. It was after she left the team when she started treating you so horribly."

Natalie thought about that for a moment. It was true. She had never really thought about the connection between Lexi's pranks and gymnastics before. But there had to be more to it than her jealousy over Natalie's gymnastics skill. That didn't seem like reason enough to end a friendship.

"She told me once that she knew she wasn't good enough for the Olympics, but she really wanted to get a college scholarship for gymnastics someday," Olivia told them.

Trinity nodded. "That's what she told me too."

"She never told me that." Natalie was surprised. "Why didn't you guys ever mention it before?"

"I guess I thought you knew," Olivia replied. "I never thought about it until now, and it all just sort of clicked with what Trin was saying."

"I feel kind of bad for her," Trinity admitted.

"I don't." Olivia's bitter tone had returned. "She's made all the wrong choices. Now, she's going to have to deal with the consequences."

Natalie couldn't bring herself to be bitter toward Lexi. Instead, she longed to understand her, to know what had caused the change in her. And though there was only a miniscule chance she would leave Virginia Beach with the answers she sought, she still prayed that she would.

The girls headed back toward the resort, walking along the boardwalk. Rays of sunlight peeked through the clouds to the west as the sun dropped lower, leaving the eastern sky with a cotton candy pink glow. They stopped near the statue of Neptune, and Natalie gazed out toward the water at the choppy waves.

"I'm cold. I'm heading back," Trinity announced.

Olivia began to follow her.

"Liv," Natalie called after them. "Can we talk?"

Trinity motioned toward the resort and kept walking. "I'll see you at the room."

Olivia slowly shuffled her way back to Natalie, and the two of them sat down together on the sand.

"I'm really sorry I've been so wrapped up in myself this week, Liv."

Olivia sighed. "I had all these expectations for how the week was going to be, and then you weren't on the bus coming down here, and everything's been happening for you with Colton. I was just really disappointed."

"I'm sorry. I didn't know any of that was going to happen."

"I know," Olivia replied. "It's not your fault. I blame Colton completely."

Natalie laughed. "So do I."

"I'm happy for you, Natty. I am. But I have some big news I need to tell you about. I've been trying to get it out every day, but there hasn't been a good time to tell you."

"You can tell me now." Natalie turned to face Olivia, giving her the full, undivided attention she deserved.

"I've been accepted to the Pratt Institute in New York for the fall semester," Olivia announced.

Natalie didn't know what to say at first.

"I'm going to study architecture." Olivia couldn't hold back her smile.

"I didn't even know you applied to Pratt," Natalie replied, unable to contain her surprise.

"I applied last fall," she admitted.

"Why didn't you tell me any of this before?"

Olivia pressed her lips together. "I was afraid."

"Liv, why?"

"We've had this plan for so long to go to Arizona and room together. I know how excited you are about it, and I was too. I loved the idea of going to college with you, spending four more years together. But deep down I knew it wasn't where I wanted to be, and I didn't want to disappoint you."

The fact that Olivia felt the need to hide this from her made her heart ache.

"Olivia, you're my best friend in the entire world, and I want nothing more than for you to be happy. If Pratt makes you happy and you get to study something you love, then I could never be disappointed about that. And I would never want to hold you back from what you're meant to do. I want you to live your best possible life, just like you've always encouraged me to do."

"Really?" Olivia asked with such hope in her voice.

"Of course." Natalie hugged her best friend with all her might. "I'll miss you in Arizona, though, Liv."

Olivia gave her a tight squeeze. "I'll miss you too."

Back in their room, Natalie stood on the balcony staring out at the dark night sky, listening to the sounds of the ocean below. She took a seat in one of the deck chairs and opened her text messages. Her thumb hovered over Colton's name. She told herself she wouldn't reach out to him, and she'd done so well at sticking to her resolve, but the entire day felt empty without him.

She tapped his name and started to type, then stopped. No matter how much she wanted to talk to him, nothing had changed. She was about to close her phone when she noticed the tell-tale dots bouncing on her screen, a sign that Colton was typing. Her heart leapt into her throat.

Cole:
Hey.

                                                  Nat:
                                                Hi.

Cole:
How was your day?

                                                Nat:
                                It was a day.

Cole:
Same here.
Sucked not seeing you.

                                                Nat:
                                Agreed.

The three little dots bounced for quite a while before Colton's next message came through.

Cole:
I just want you to know that I respect where you're coming from. I do. I couldn't stand it today, not talking to you, not seeing you, because this thing between us is special. You're special. I meant what I said in the car. You're more real to me than anyone else in my life right now. If all we can ever be is friends, I will accept that, as long as you're in my life.

Tears sprang to Natalie's eyes. She felt the same. There *was* something special between them.

Nat:
I want you in my life too.

25
Trust

I t's supposed to rain today," Trinity announced with annoyance in her voice as she stared at the day's forecast on the local morning news program. "I came here for the beach. Why won't the rain stay away?"

Natalie wandered to the sliding glass door. The ocean was churning with waves, and the sky was dark in the distance. She could see the rain dropping from the clouds far out over the water. She slid the door open and a blast of sticky, humid air blew her hair back.

"Shut the door!" Olivia hollered from her place still in bed.

"Sorry." Natalie shoved it closed and turned her attention to the meteorologist on the television.

"Looks like we're in for some storms, folks." He pointed at the cluster of reds and yellows on the radar and reported an eighty percent chance of thunderstorms throughout the day with the possibility of some becoming severe in the evening.

Natalie immediately tensed up. She had woken with a smile and a fresh perspective. All was well with Olivia again. She and Colton were determined to be part of each other's lives. And she was one day away from her eighteenth birthday. She thought nothing could possibly ruin her happy mood. Until she saw that forecast.

"So much for a day at the beach," Trinity said.

Rain pelted the windows of the hotel restaurant as the girls ate their lunch. Natalie still shivered when the thunder boomed, but she tried to focus on her nice memory of Colton from the last storm they had encountered.

She took a bite of caesar salad, and her phone rang.

"Hey, Dad."

"Hey, Natty Gann." His nickname for her from the movie they watched often when she was a kid. "Are you ready to come home yet?"

"Today, I could probably be persuaded." She chomped on a crouton.

"Why, what's the matter?"

"Storms." Her dad understood her fear of storms. Many nights, he had knelt by her bed and prayed her through them.

"Ah, I see. Are you OK, sweetie?"

"I'm fine, Dad. How's everything there? How's my car?"

"Car's in the shop. But the good news is it should be ready by the time you get back."

"Awesome." She took a deep breath. "Are you still mad?"

"I wasn't mad. Not at you anyway. I was more worried about you."

"I know."

"I'm just glad that boy got you to the school. I was nervous the entire time thinking about you riding with him when he caused your accident."

Her stomach sank.

"If I never see him again it will be too soon."

She had to come clean. She couldn't hide it anymore. "Dad, there's something I need to tell you."

"Sounds serious. Everything all right?"

"Colton gave me a ride here." She spit the words out as quickly as she could.

Trinity and Olivia stopped eating and stared at her.

"I know he did," her dad replied.

"No, not to the bus." She held her breath. "To Virginia."

"Wait, what? What do you mean? You didn't ride the bus down there?" The volume of his voice raised with each question.

She could picture the surprise and disappointment on her father's face, and it broke her heart. "We missed the bus, Dad."

"Natalie Jean Rhodes!"

She held the phone away from her head, and her friends' eyes widened.

"You better be joking with me right now!"

169

"It's no joke." Natalie left the table and walked out into the resort lobby. "We missed the bus."

"Why didn't you call and tell me that? I told you to call me if you missed the bus. We would've figured out a way to get you there."

"Dad, it was his fault I missed the bus in the first place, and he offered to pay for gas and food for the drive down. He felt really bad."

"He *should* feel bad. This is unacceptable."

"But I made it safe and sound. I'm here. Can't we just let it go?"

Her dad was quiet for a few beats. "You lied to me, Natalie. You know how I feel about that."

Natalie hung her head. "I know, Daddy. I'm sorry." Her voice was tinged with shame.

"I have a mind to drive down there and get you right now."

"I'm coming home on the bus in two days."

"You better be on that bus, young lady." His end of the phone was quiet again. "I'm very disappointed in you."

"What did I do that was so wrong? Besides lie to you, I mean."

He let out an exasperated breath. "Where do I start?"

"I'm eighteen tomorrow, Dad." She decided to play the adult card. "It's time I make my own decisions, don't you think?"

"This lack of good judgment shows that you're clearly not capable of that yet."

"I'm an adult in the eyes of the law."

"Speaking of the law, that boy took our underaged daughter out of the state without our consent."

Natalie didn't reply at first. She knew he was right.

"I'm not surprised he would do such a thing, but you ... I can't believe you did this."

"You're not going to get Colton into trouble, are you?" It had been one of her biggest concerns when it came to telling her dad the truth.

"I could."

"Dad, please don't," she begged. "I would be humiliated."

"Maybe you should've thought about that before."

"Dad, I'm sorry."

"I thought I could trust you." His voice was quiet and sad.

"You can, Daddy. You can."

"I'm not so sure anymore."

Tears stung her eyes.

"I need to get back to work."

"I love you, Dad."

There was a long pause before he responded with, "I love you too."

Her heart broke at the sound of their call ending. She hadn't meant to lose her father's trust. She hadn't meant for any of this to happen. What if her relationship with her father was damaged irreparably?

Her appetite was lost, so she headed back to the room and threw herself down on her bed. The tears would not stop, and she let them flow, praying her dad would forgive her for lying to him.

Regretful and emotionally drained, sleep overcame her.

Storms were always worse at night, and the one brewing outside was preventing her from falling asleep. That and the fact that she was wide awake because of her unexpected nap earlier. She squeezed her eyes closed, but it didn't stop her from seeing every flash of lightning through her eyelids. And covering her ears with her hands did nothing to shut out the loud, rolling thunder as the storm grew near. Her friends were sound asleep while she gripped her pillow as tightly as she could, praying for sleep to come.

As another round of thunder rumbled, she heard a strange buzzing sound and realized it was her phone vibrating on the nightstand next to her head. She opened her eyes long enough to see that it was Colton trying to FaceTime her, and she tapped the screen to answer.

"Are you OK?" he asked before she even had a chance to speak. His handsome face was distorted by the cracks across her screen.

"Not really." She laid the phone sideways on her pillow next to her head and lowered the volume so she wouldn't wake the girls.

"I wish I could come over there right now."

She whimpered as the thunder cracked loudly, and she almost gave in and told him to come.

Colton cleared his throat and hummed. He then proceeded to sing her the first verse of "I Can't Help Falling in Love With You", like he had in the tent that night.

Natalie smiled into the phone, though it was dark in her room, and she wasn't sure the light from her phone was enough for him to see her. He was the sweetest, most thoughtful guy on the entire planet.

"Does that help?" he asked when he had finished.

"It helped." She honestly felt calmer just knowing he cared, knowing how concerned he was about her.

"Wish I could calm you down the way I did last time."

"Colton." She couldn't let on that she had been thinking the same thing.

"Well, I do. I'm just being honest."

She was thankful that the darkness hid her grin.

"Hey, it's after midnight now," he said.

"So."

"So ... happy birthday."

He was right. She was now eighteen.

He held the phone closer to his face and smiled. "I'm glad I was the first to say it."

"Thank you."

"So now if the cops pull us over, I don't have to worry about getting arrested."

Natalie giggled at that.

"I'll let you get some sleep now."

"Wait, I wanted you to know that I told my dad."

His eyes widened. "You did? How did he take it?"

"Not good."

She could see him hang his head a little. "He hates me now, doesn't he?"

"He was angrier with me for lying to him."

"I'm sure he'll forgive you," he said.

"I hope so." Her throat tightened at the thought of her relationship with her dad being forever broken.

"Hey, can we hang out later? I have a gift for you."

"You didn't have to get me anything." But knowing that he had warmed her heart.

"I wanted to."

"That's sweet."

"Well, you know me." He gave her the cute dimple smile.

Her stomach fluttered. She couldn't help it. The way he smiled at her was everything.

"So, I'll see you later then?" he asked.

"Yeah."

"Goodnight, Nat." His phone began to turn away.

"Colton ..."

"Yeah?" He faced the camera again.

"Thank you for calling."

He nodded. "Of course."

"Goodnight."

"Night."

26
Calming the Storm

ighteen years old. Natalie woke with a hopeful feeling after her phone call with Colton. She had no idea what the future held. Heck, she had no idea what the day held even, but she knew good things were coming.

She sat up in bed and stretched. Glancing around the room, she noticed streamers and balloons and colorfully wrapped packages on the table. She slowly crawled out of bed and walked over to see the pile of gifts and cards from her friends. She wasn't sure how they had dragged themselves out of bed to do all of this or how they did it without waking her, but she loved it.

Natalie walked to the sliding glass door and slid the curtain back enough to open the door and step outside onto the balcony. The weather was still gloomy and literal grey clouds hung over her special day, but she wouldn't let it dampen her spirits. She was determined to enjoy every moment of her birthday.

"Good morning." Olivia peeked out the door behind her.

"Morning, Liv."

Olivia joined her on the balcony and wrapped an arm around her. "Happy birthday."

Natalie leaned her head on Olivia's shoulder. "Thank you. The decorations are so pretty. How did you do that with me sleeping?"

"Very, very carefully." She giggled.

They stared out at the waves beating against the sand, and Natalie realized this truly was their last hurrah. Once they returned home, there would be finals to take, graduation to prepare for, open houses to attend, summer jobs to work. The next three months would go by in a flash, and they would go their separate ways.

"I love you, Liv."

Olivia rested her head against Natalie's and gave her a squeeze. "I love you too."

A droplet hit Natalie's nose, and she opened her hands as rain began to fall.

"Want to open one of your gifts?" Olivia made a move toward the room.

Natalie's eyes brightened. "I want to open all of them."

The girls giggled and raced back into the room to escape the rain.

Natalie plopped down on the bed with Trinity and squeezed her leg through the blanket. "Time to get up, Trin."

Trinity groaned. "Nooo!"

"But it's my birthday."

She opened one eye and looked back over her shoulder at Natalie. "Happy birthday, Natty."

"Thanks. I want to open presents now, so get up!"

Trinity slowly rolled out of bed, and they flipped the lights on as Natalie opened Trinity's gift—a cute yellow sundress she had seen in one of the shops the other day but couldn't really afford. The other packages from Trinity were matching sandals and jewelry. Then she opened a cute scrapbook Olivia had made for her of pictures of the three of them throughout their friendship.

They sat for a while flipping through the album, reminiscing about all the good times they had shared together, laughing at the funny moments and tearing up at the sweet ones.

"Thank you both. I love all my gifts."

"There's one more," Olivia announced as she handed Natalie a card and package that had been hidden behind the chair.

Her heart skipped a beat, thinking it might be from Colton.

"This is from your Dad."

Natalie chewed on her bottom lip as she carefully took the medium rectangular package from her and ran her fingers over her name in her father's handwriting. She opened the card first with its photograph of a little girl dancing on her father's feet and a sentiment about dancing her way through life. He had added the words *and flipping* above the word *dancing*. Inside was a brief handwritten note telling her how much he loved her and would miss her when she left

175

for college in the fall. Her heart squeezed. She missed him, and she regretted keeping the whole truth about the trip from him. And when she opened the package and found a beautiful leather-bound Bible with her name embossed on the cover and a note on the dedication page that read "You will always find the truth about life within these pages", she began to cry.

"Oh, Natalie," Olivia said. "It will be OK. Your dad will come around."

"I really hurt him." She sniffled.

"He'll forgive you."

Natalie wasn't so sure.

The rain prevented the girls from doing anything outdoorsy for Natalie's birthday, so they spent the day roaming through the same shops they had already visited, having ice cream inside while staring out at the empty beach, and hanging out in the room watching TV and wasting time on their phones. Their last full day of vacation seemed like a total bust.

Olivia and Trinity insisted they all dress up and go to dinner at the resort restaurant downstairs, though Natalie didn't feel much like celebrating. But once she was in her new yellow dress with the matching sandals, her hair curled and half pulled up, and her face made up for once, her mood shifted. Amazing what a little makeup and new clothes could do to lift the spirit.

Natalie walked with confidence to the crowded restaurant, but she became unnerved when she spotted Colton and Lexi seated at a table across the room from theirs.

Olivia and Trinity both turned to see what had caused her dumbfounded expression.

"Forget about them," Trinity told her.

"Not worth it," Olivia added.

She only wished she *could* forget.

Natalie did her best to ignore them and enjoy the chicken parmesan, which reminded her of talent night at that little Italian grille. When the girls had finished eating, the waitress brought out a small cake her friends had decorated for her, complete with lit candles, and the waitstaff sang her the birthday song. She blushed the entire time. The only time she appreciated that much attention was when she was at gymnastics competitions.

"Make a wish and blow out those candles," Trinity said.

Natalie peeked over at Colton. Had he even noticed she was there? He wasn't looking at her, but his date was. Lexi's eyes were firing warning daggers in her direction. Her mind flashed to Lexi and Grant lip-locked at the amusement park and a surge of anger shot through her.

She turned back to her cake then closed her eyes. Most girls probably would've wished for Colton and Lexi to break up—she wanted that more than she was willing to admit to anyone—but it's not what she wished for as she took in a deep breath and puffed out the candles.

"So ..." Trinity said.

"So, what?"

"Your wish."

"If I tell you what I wished for, it won't come true."

Trinity let out a little snort. "That's a bunch of bull."

Natalie simply shook her head and smiled.

"Won't you even tell *me* what you wished for?"

Natalie's head jerked to the left when she heard Colton's voice. There was still a twinge of pain in her neck from the accident, but she didn't care. Colton was standing over her, his hand resting on her shoulder.

She smiled up at him. "Not even you."

"Happy birthday." His smile lit up his face. "You look beautiful."

"Thanks." A blush colored her cheeks.

"Like you were meant to ride in my car."

Natalie glanced down at the yellow of her dress and smiled.

"Did you have a good day?"

She shrugged. *Getting better.* She couldn't stop smiling.

"Can we meet up after dinner to talk?"

"Sure."

He smiled the most adorable smile at her. "Cool. I'll text you when I'm done here."

She nodded.

He squeezed her shoulder then walked back across the restaurant to Lexi, who looked ready to breathe fire.

Olivia cut a slice of cake for Natalie and placed it in front of her. "Oh my gosh. You two are so smitten."

"What?" Natalie feigned innocence.

"You have a permasmile." She cut a piece for Trinity.

"I can't help it." She pressed her lips together, trying to stop the smile from spreading, but she failed.

"Eat your cake." Olivia pointed to her plate.

"Yes, ma'am."

Natalie took a bite of red velvet cake with the creamiest white frosting. Her eyes practically rolled back in her head. "Oh, that's really, really—"

Her praise of the cake was suddenly interrupted by the sound of glass breaking, followed by yelling— well, more like shrieking.

"Are you serious?" Lexi stood next to their table, yelling at Colton. "You're doing this now?"

Natalie couldn't hear Colton's response, but he reached for her arm, trying to get her to sit down, and she batted his hand away.

Lexi's gaze suddenly fell on Natalie, and before she knew it, Lexi was making a beeline for her.

"You!" Lexi shouted. "You did this!"

Colton was on her heels.

"I did nothing." Natalie knew Lexi probably wouldn't believe anything she said, but the desire to defend herself kicked in.

Lexi wagged a finger at her. "I told you to keep your mouth shut. You're going to be so sorry for this."

"I didn't tell him."

"Tell me what?" Colton's eyes flew from Natalie's to Lexi's.

There was panic in Lexi's eyes. "Nothing."

"What are you talking about?" He looked at Natalie again. "Tell me."

Natalie shook her head slightly, afraid to break the news, afraid of what Lexi might do.

His expression was almost as serious as it had been when Natalie accidentally called him *king*. "One of you better tell me right now."

"She's been cheating on you with Grant," Trinity squeaked out.

"Trinity!" Natalie and Olivia both spoke at the same time.

"Come on. He deserves to know."

The color left Colton's face for an instant, then rushed back with a force. He clenched his jaw, muscles twitching, eyes narrowing at Lexi. "How could you do that?" He shook his head in astonishment. "How could *he* do that?"

"I'm sorry, Colt. Please. Please don't leave me." Tears sprung to Lexi's eyes.

"We're already through. I told you."

Natalie's heart sped up. *He finally broke up with her?* It was awful that he had found out about Lexi's indiscretion this way, but joy rushed through her, knowing he had already ended things.

Colton's eyes met hers, and she saw pain and confusion there. A sinking feeling in her stomach replaced the flutters of joy she had felt only moments before.

"Why didn't you tell me?" he whispered.

"I'm sorry," she replied quietly.

"How long have you known?"

Natalie hesitated. "A couple days."

The hurt in his eyes was unmistakable. "You should've told me."

"I didn't think it was my place."

He looked from her to Lexi and back again. "I have to go."

As soon as he was ten steps away, Lexi sank to the floor next to Natalie's legs and began to weep. In that moment, Natalie's heart went out to her. Despite her terrible choices, she was still a girl with feelings, and Natalie had a strong urge to help her.

"Are you all right?" Natalie laid a hand on her shoulder.

Lexi's hand shot up and grabbed her wrist. Her eyes fixed on the wall of windows overlooking the ocean, and she bolted to her feet with Natalie's wrist in a death grip.

"*Ow!* Lexi! Let go!" she cried.

Lexi yanked her up from the seat. "You're coming with me."

"What, where?" She attempted to twist her wrist out of Lexi's hold, but she was overpowered.

"Lexi!" Olivia and Trinity both cried, following after them.

Lexi acted as if she hadn't heard them and continued to drag

Natalie through the restaurant, past the other patrons, and through the french doors that opened onto the patio.

The rain was coming down in sheets and soaked the girls within seconds. Natalie began to shake as lightning illuminated the sky.

"Lexi, please!" she cried.

"Let her go!" Trinity called from the patio doors.

"Lexi, come on!" Olivia yelled after them.

Still Lexi walked, down the steps to the beach, dragging Natalie along.

The thunder boomed and shook Natalie to her core. She tripped and fell onto the sand. Lexi pulled on her arm, trying to get her to stand.

"Get up!"

"Where are you taking me?" She was breathing heavily from the struggle, and her head was starting to pound.

"We're going for a swim, like when we were kids. And I know how much you love thunderstorms."

"Please stop," Natalie begged.

"I thought we'd relive the best days of our friendship. Remember how we'd swim for hours in Gun Lake until our fingers were all pruned up. Remember your mom always called us her little fishies." Lexi stopped speaking then, her gaze connecting with Natalie's.

Natalie stared up at her. The memory of her mother calling them that rushed back.

Lexi finally dropped her arm and continued on toward the water. "You're not the only one who lost a mom, you know?" Lexi shouted as she neared the turbulent waters.

Natalie could see she was crying and ran after her, pushing aside her fear of the storm. "Lexi, you can't go in the water right now. Not with all this lightning. The waves are too big. It's too dangerous!" She moved faster toward her. "I'm sorry you lost your mom. I loved her too."

"I'm not talking about *my* mom!" She was nearing the water's edge.

"Stop! Lexi, stop!" Natalie caught up to her and grabbed hold of her arms, yanking her away from the water.

"You always take everything from me!" Lexi screamed and spun toward her. "I can't take it anymore!"

"So, you're just going to drown yourself?" Natalie cried over another boom of thunder.

"It's better than the alternative."

"Better than life?"

Lexi broke down then, and Natalie was able to lead her farther up onto the beach, where she collapsed onto her knees.

Natalie sat down in the sand next to her. "Come on, Lex. Talk to me."

"Your mom was like a mother to me," Lexi whimpered. "Especially after my mom died. She was there, loving me like I was her own daughter. And then she betrayed us, and I didn't think I could ever look at her the same way again."

"Betrayed us?"

"When she slept with my dad."

Natalie's mouth dropped along with her stomach. "Your dad?"

Lexi's brow furrowed. "You didn't know?"

Natalie could only shake her head in response. *He* was the man her mom had cheated with? No wonder Dad had been so upset. Lexi's dad was one of his closest friends.

"Things were just different after that," Lexi explained. "It was too hard to be around you, knowing what had happened between our parents, so I quit gymnastics and stayed away. I never planned to stay away forever, though. I needed time to figure stuff out. But then your mom left, and I was so angry and hurt and confused. I was just as devastated as you were, and I needed you, but you weren't around anymore. Your whole life became about gymnastics."

"Gymnastics helped me get through her leaving."

"You hid away at that gym so you wouldn't have to deal with her not being home anymore. And I felt abandoned—by your mom *and* by you.

Natalie's heart broke. "You never told me any of that."

"I didn't know how."

If she had, things might have turned out very differently. "So instead, you and your friends tortured me?"

"I wanted you to hurt like I was hurting." Lexi stared down and grabbed a handful of wet sand, letting it fall in a clump by her knees.

"Lex."

"I chose Colton because of you, ya know." Lexi still wouldn't make eye contact with Natalie.

"What do you mean?"

"I mean, you've liked him since we were six, and I thought it would hurt the most if I got the guy you always wanted. Looks like the joke's on me. You still get the guy, and I'm left alone again."

"You're not alone, Lexi. I meant what I said the other day. I never stopped caring about you and missing our friendship."

Lexi looked at her then. "You're just saying that."

"No, I'm not." Natalie pulled her into an embrace, tears burning her eyes. Lexi didn't make a move to reciprocate the hug at first, but still she held on.

Several minutes passed before Lexi finally tightened her arms around Natalie. "I'm really sorry, Natty." Her voice cracked with emotion.

Natalie's heart filled with happiness to hear Lexi call her that again.

"I know you could never forgive me for all the horrific things I've done, but I *am* sorry."

Natalie let go and looked her in the eyes. "You were hurting, and I didn't know it. Of course, I forgive you."

"But ... how could you?"

"Because I still remember the old Lexi. The one who spent every waking moment at our house. The one who was like the sister I always wanted. And I believe you're still that girl deep down."

"I want to be."

Natalie smiled at her.

Lexi smiled weakly then lowered her head. "I did love Colton, you know. I didn't mean to fall for Grant. I didn't mean for things to go as far with him as they did, but Colton's been distant for months, and I could feel him pulling away. I don't know if he'll ever be able to forgive us."

"I think he will. In time."

"Natalie!" Olivia and Trinity stood just inside the patio doors, waving their arms, waiting.

"We should go in." Natalie stood and held her hand out to Lexi.

Lexi took it and stood. "Hey ... it's still storming and you don't seem scared anymore."

Natalie glanced up at the sky. It was the strangest thing. The thunder was still cracking. The lightning was still flashing. But she was no longer shaking. All she felt was a sense of relief. "Weird."

"Natalie!" Olivia and Trinity cried again.

Natalie and Lexi began to walk toward the restaurant. "Will you come back to our room and have some cake for my birthday?"

Lexi's eyes filled with tears again. "I'd like that." She looked down at herself. "I might need to change first."

Natalie looked at her own dress, soaked through and covered in sand. "Me too."

27
Eighteen Hours

Bright morning light filled the room and roused Natalie from her slumber. She glanced over her shoulder at Lexi, who had fallen asleep in their room last night after many hours of talking and eating cake. Having Lexi there with them was strange at first, considering it had been six years since any of them had been friends with her. Olivia and Trinity hadn't seemed convinced by Lexi's sudden change of heart. Who could blame them after all Natalie had suffered because of her?

After an hour of awkward small talk had passed, the conversation shifted to more difficult topics—the betrayal by Natalie's mom and the bullying. Natalie hadn't meant for the past to come up again after their conversation on the beach. Things felt settled to her. She felt closure there. But it had been Lexi who wanted to clear the air. And the more they all talked—the more Lexi admitted to her wrongdoings and apologized—the clearer it became that she was truly sorry.

Looking at their situation from the outside, one might've wondered how on earth Natalie could forgive Lexi. But sitting in the middle of that storm, she saw Lexi for who she was—a brokenhearted girl who had lost not only one mom but two, who felt abandoned by her best friend, who struck out at others to mask the pain she had never dealt with. And in that moment, forgiveness had been a simple decision, one Natalie knew in her heart was the right choice. After all, God had forgiven her for all the stupid things she had done in her life, including all the lies she had told on this trip. Forgiving Lexi seemed infinitesimal in light of that.

The clock read 6:30 a.m. when Natalie rolled out of bed. One last morning on the balcony. She stepped out with her phone in hand, hoping to see a message from Colton, but there was nothing. Opening the camera roll on her phone, she scrolled through pictures from the week, stopping on the ones of her and Colton together. She scrolled back to the road trip and stared at the picture she had secretly taken of Colton walking along the path at Brandywine Falls. Her heart ached.

In a matter of hours, she would leave with her bags packed and loaded onto the bus, and Colton would go back on his own. Not knowing where they stood unnerved her almost as much as storms usually did.

Natalie leaned against the railing and admired the warm glow of sunrise, thankful the bad weather had finally pushed through during the night and made way for a beautiful, cloudless sky. If only she could see the hope of a brand new day so clearly, but a dark cloud of uncertainty obstructed her view.

She stayed outside for a long time, thinking, going over everything that had happened, until she heard her friends moving within. It was time to get ready, have a little breakfast, then pack for the trip home. She glimpsed her phone once more before returning to the room, willing a text to appear. Nada.

Lexi was sitting on the end of Natalie's bed when she entered. She was checking her phone too, but unlike Natalie, she was smiling.

"Is it Grant?" Natalie asked.

Lexi nodded, unable to contain her happiness.

"I'm happy for you." Natalie rifled through her suitcase for something comfortable to wear for the trip home.

"Natalie."

She looked over at Lexi.

"I'm glad we talked." Lexi pressed her lips together and looked like she was holding back tears again. There had been plenty of those during the talk last night.

"So am I," Natalie replied.

"All of us." Lexi looked at Olivia then Trinity.

Trinity sat up and stretched her arms above her head. "Me too."

"Me three," Olivia added.

"I still feel so bad about everything, though." Lexi lowered her head sadly.

Olivia and Trinity moved to sit next to her on the bed and put their arms around her. Natalie climbed up behind them and wrapped her arms around the bunch, resting her chin on Lexi's shoulder.

"Like we said last night," Natalie said. "It's all in the past."

Lexi shook her head in disbelief. "I don't know what I did to deserve your forgiveness or your friendship, but I'll take it."

"You've got it," Natalie replied.

After breakfast, the girls parted ways and returned to their rooms to pack their things, just making it out by the checkout time of eleven o'clock. They walked out onto the sidewalk with rolling suitcases, juggling bags in their arms and over their shoulders, on their way to the buses.

"Natalie!"

She closed her eyes and smiled at the sound of Colton's voice. A rush of happiness spread through her as she turned to see him jogging toward them.

"Can we talk before you go?" he asked.

"Of course." She turned to the girls. "I'll catch up with you."

Olivia and Trinity both smiled at her knowingly as they left.

"I didn't know if I'd hear from you today or not." Her gaze followed her friends across the parking lot to the bus.

"I just needed a little time to process things. It was kind of a shock."

"Yeah, I know." She set her bags down. "I'm sorry I didn't tell you when I found out."

"You were right," he replied. "It should've been them to tell me."

"Did you talk to them yet?" she asked.

"I confronted Grant last night. He admitted it." Colton shook his head. "He said he's in love with her."

"She's in love with him too."

Colton's mouth formed into an *O*. "Did she tell you that?"

"Not in so many words, but yeah. I'm pretty sure she feels the same."

"I'm more upset about the betrayal than anything, but I don't think I really have the right to be mad about it. I did the same thing. With you." He gave her a little smile.

"Well … not exactly the same thing."

He chuckled. "Hey, if they want to be together, great. They deserve each other. But the way they went about it was wrong."

"Actually, Lexi and I had a little breakthrough last night after you left."

"Really?"

"We kind of cleared the air. About a lot of things. And I think we might actually be friends again."

"Wow!" His eyes widened. "That's unexpected. But it's a good thing, right?"

She nodded. "You should really talk to her. She feels pretty bad about how things went down."

"I will." He reached out and touched her arm. "But not today."

The nerve endings in Natalie's arm sent a tingling sensation over her skin.

His eyes met hers. "Today, I want to talk to you."

"What about?" She acted coy.

"I never got to give you your birthday gift."

Natalie smiled. "Oh, right."

He retrieved a small rectangular package with a tiny pink bow from behind his back. "Happy birthday, Natalie."

Nerves settled in her stomach as she peeled back the wrapping paper and opened the box within to reveal a white gold bracelet with several charms attached.

"May I?" Colton lifted the bracelet from the box and unhooked the clasp.

Goosebumps spread over her skin as his fingertips gently took her arm and lifted her wrist, wrapping the bracelet around and clasping it securely. He held her wrist in his hand and lifted one of the charms—a tiny green tent. "To remember our trip."

She smiled at that and reached for the bracelet, turning it to see the other charms—the silhouette of a gymnast, a football, a banjo, a tiny yellow sports car.

She eyed the next charm. "A clown hat?" She raised her eyebrows at him.

He shrugged. "It was the closest thing I could find to a ventriloquist dummy."

Natalie laughed loudly. "That's not the same thing at all."

"I'll take it back then."

She swatted his hand away when he reached for it. "You'll just have to take me to the circus."

"Clowns don't creep you out?"

"Not really." She turned the bracelet some more and saw a silver bolt of lightning. Her eyes met his. "I love it. Thank you."

Colton took her hands in his. "I have to say something. And I need you to hear me out before you say anything."

"All right," she replied.

"Remember what I said at the campground? 'What if our accident was no accident?'"

She nodded.

"I was stopped at that intersection on Saturday. Completely stopped. The sun wasn't in my eyes. I saw your car coming, and I had no intention of pulling out in front of you. At all. My foot was firmly on that brake."

Natalie's forehead creased in confusion.

"But then something happened. Something strange that I still can't quite explain." He shook his head a little. "My car started moving forward. Like, I was stepping on the brake, but it was still going. So I gunned it, because if I hadn't, you probably would've crashed right into the side of my car, and maybe we'd both be dead right now."

Natalie's eyes widened, and her heart rate picked up.

"Before I left the house that morning, I was sitting alone in my room, not sure if I wanted to go at all. I was confused and kind of annoyed about life, and I did something I never do ... I prayed.

"I haven't prayed since I was a little kid at Neil's church. Ever since Chris, I've been going through life in a daze, just doing whatever I wanted, whatever made me feel good, trying to ignore the pain, trying to ignore this little voice in my head that kept telling me to turn away from all that stuff.

"Something changed in me the day I went back to that church six months ago. I knew it. I felt it. And I've been fighting it ever since. Until the morning of the accident. That's when I told God that I believe in Him and I trust Him, and I asked Him for three things.

"First, that I would find the right time to end my relationship with Lexi. Second, that He would show me very clearly the path I'm meant to take in this life and give me the strength to take it, even if that means going against my dad. And then I asked for someone to travel that path with.

"Like I told you, Lexi and I have been over for a while. I just didn't know how to end it. So I'm kinda relieved she and Grant want to be together, because I really didn't want to hurt her. And now I feel like we can all move on.

"All of the things we talked about—the mission trip, me going to college for something other than what my dad wants, making my own path rather than following in his footsteps—everything you said to me just confirmed that it's what I'm supposed to do. I looked up Sports Medicine degrees at MSU. They're under the Kinesiology Department." He winked at her.

"So we'll be studying the same thing." She smiled at him.

"I never would've decided to go for it without your advice."

Colton reached into his pocket, revealing another charm—a small pink heart—and attached it to the bracelet.

His eyes told Natalie exactly what he was going to say before he said the words. He leaned forward until his forehead was touching hers.

"You're the one, Natalie," he said. "My answer to prayer. Although, I had no idea when I prayed about traveling life's path that we would literally go on a trip together."

Natalie let out a little laugh and leaned back to look up at him.

He let go of her hands, his fingertips skimming along her arms on their way to her face.

A delightful warmth took over her body as his fingers moved along each side of her neck and slid into her hair, his thumbs softly brushing her cheeks. "Will you ride home with me?"

His smile melted her heart. She hadn't expected him to ask, but part of her had hoped he would. But before she could answer, there was something she knew she had to do.

"I have to tell my dad."

"I already did," he replied.

"You talked to my dad?" This was a twist.

"I apologized for the accident and for my part in getting you to take the road trip down here with me."

"What did he say?"

"He seemed angry at first, but when I told him what I just told you about the accident, he calmed down, and we had a good talk about faith and stuff."

Natalie let out a sigh of relief.

"I also asked if I could drive you home."

"You did? What did he say to that?" She knew what the answer probably was.

Colton let go of her face, pulled his phone from his back pocket, and made a call. "Hello, sir … yes, she's right here." He held the phone out to Natalie.

She took it hesitantly. "Hello?"

"I'm sorry we fought, Natty," her dad said.

Her heart squeezed. "Me too, Daddy."

"It's hard for a father to let go of his precious girl, you know. I was afraid you lying to me was a sign that you were on the wrong path, that maybe nothing I had ever taught you had sunk in."

"I know. I made a mistake."

"But you told me the truth, and I'm proud of you for that. And I want you to know that I *do* trust you. I trust you to make your own decisions. You're a smart girl, and I know you would never put yourself at risk. But I worry. That's what parents do. You're going to be on your own soon, and I guess I need to start working on this whole letting go thing."

Tears sprang to Natalie's eyes. "I'm so sorry, Dad. I'll never lie to you again."

"I know you won't."

Her father rarely cried in front of her, but she could've sworn she heard a sniffle on his end of the line.

"Be safe," he said. "Don't let him drive too fast, and no staying in the same hotel room together."

She was so happy that she thought her heart might burst. "We're friends, Dad."

He snickered. "Have you told *him* that?"

"Dad."

"Just remember what you've been taught. Remember what I wrote in your birthday gift."

"I will. Thank you for that, by the way. It's beautiful, and I love it." She couldn't wait to see him, so she could give him a huge hug and tell him to his face how much the gift meant to her.

"I hope you'll take it with you to Arizona, and let it be your guide."

"I will."

"Happy birthday, sweet girl."

"I love you, Dad."

"I love you too."

She was crying as the call ended, and she handed the phone back to Colton. He tucked it in his back pocket and wrapped his arms around her, letting her cry until the tears subsided.

"Your dad seems great." Colton took her face in his hands again and wiped away her tears with his thumbs.

"He's the best." She sniffled.

"So what do you say? Will you go with me?" He gazed into her eyes. "There's no one else I'd rather travel eighteen hours with than you."

A smile spread across Natalie's face, and she nodded slightly.

"Is that a yes?" His eyebrows raised hopefully.

"Yes."

Colton brought her into his arms and pressed his lips to her forehead. "Awesome."

She giggled at that.

He leaned back and gazed into her eyes.

She knew what was coming next, and her stomach fluttered in anticipation.

Colton leaned forward and touched his lips to hers for several soft kisses, smiling against her lips between each one.

"I've been wanting to do that since the day we got here," he whispered in that intimate way she loved.

"I've been wanting you to."

He leaned in for more, kissing her like a guy who'd been holding back for a week.

Natalie tightened her arms around his waist and melted into him, returning his kisses, letting him know there was nowhere else in the world she'd rather be.

His kisses slowed, turning soft and tender again, and she clung to him, afraid her knees might give out when he stopped.

She couldn't stop smiling, and neither could he.

"This is what you wished for, isn't it?" he asked with that signature confidence of his.

"I can't tell you."

He placed a soft kiss on her lips. "Yeah, you can."

"Actually, I wished that no matter what happened, no matter where we both went after this week and after graduation, that you would find your happiness."

His smile turned to a disapproving look. "You're supposed to wish for something for yourself."

"Says who?"

"Says everyone who's ever blown out their birthday candles."

"Well, I'm just a more selfless person than everyone else, I guess."

"Oh, is that so?" He grinned at her.

She nodded.

He reached up and brushed his thumb across her cheek. "Your wish came true. I found my happiness when I found you."

Her heart filled with more love than she had ever known, and she leaned in and kissed him again.

A *honk* from across the parking lot startled them, and they turned to see Olivia and Trinity exiting their bus.

"Sorry!" Trinity called over her shoulder at the bus driver, who didn't look happy with her for honking the horn.

The girls giggled as they ran up and wrapped their arms around Natalie and Colton and said their farewells.

"Bye, you two." Trinity squeezed them hard.

"Have a safe trip," Olivia said.

"How did you know?" Natalie asked.

"We know you." Olivia leaned into Natalie and gave her a kiss on the cheek.

The girls waved as they returned to the bus, and Natalie's heart warmed. There were no two greater friends in the world, and she was lucky to have them as hers.

Colton wound his fingers through hers and grabbed her suitcase with his other hand. "Where to first?" he asked as they walked toward his car.

"I don't care where we go, really, as long as we're together." She smiled sweetly at him.

His smile brought out the dimple she loved so much, but then his face straightened. "I'm not sure I should let you ride in my car again after the terrible name you called her."

"Well, I may have been a little hasty," she replied with a wink.

"Oh, really?"

"I've decided I don't hate yellow cars so much after all."

Acknowledgments

This book was totally inspired by my daughter's class trip to Cedar Point. Waiting for the buses that morning, my mind ran away with itself, wondering what would happen if a couple of the kids missed the bus, thinking about all the teenaged drivers squealing their tires when they pull out of the parking lot at the end of the school day, putting those elements together.

The story came to me pretty quickly, and it was so much fun to write, but it's SO much better because of my critique girls—Anita, Crystal, Franky, Melanie, Rachel, and Vicki. I feel so blessed to know you and so honored that you all took the time to help make my little book the best it could be. You're all so talented and insightful and wonderful. I could just go on and on.

Thanks to my wonderful Launch Team, for reading and sharing and just being there. Your help is so appreciated, and I can't thank you enough.

There would be no books if not for my hubby and kids and my mom, who offer me endless support and love and inspire me.

And thank you, sweet reader friend. I hope you enjoyed Natalie and Colton's road trip and pray their journey touched your heart.

Happy reading!

Krista

An excerpt from

the
TRUTH
about

Before

A part of me always knew there was something different about Drew. I can't even remember the first time I met him, but it seemed he was always in my life, as far back as I could recall. Maybe even longer.

One of my earliest memories of Drew was a Spring afternoon in the third grade. The sun shone brightly, warming the afternoon air, birds chirped in the trees along the edge of the playground, and we tried to swing high enough to touch the sky with our feet.

Drew reached over and grabbed my hand and it was like a surge of energy flowed between us. He had this twinkle in his eye, playful yet serious. I felt a rush of excitement, but also a sense of peace at the same time. It was a strange contradiction of emotions that I had never felt before.

We pushed off the ground and laughed joyfully, leaning back and pushing our feet as high as they would go. The wind whipped through my long, wavy hair and I felt so happy, like together we could do anything.

The shrill sound of the teacher's whistle quickly ended our perfect moment. When our swings slowed, Drew stood in front of me and took both of my hands in his as he helped me up.

"We were meant to be friends, Claire." He looked straight into my eyes, into my soul. "A friend loveth at all times."

I was used to him speaking in his "fancy talk".

"At all times," he repeated.

I smiled at him and, as usual, had nothing fancy to reply with. At that age, I was too young to understand all of his quotes, clichés and Bible verses.

"You're my best friend," I replied.

A huge smile broke out on his face. He crossed his arms over his chest in an "X", which I later learned means "love" in sign language.

Then he reached down and retrieved the brown leather notebook he carried with him always.

I never really thought much of that notebook back then. It was an extension of him, always slung over his shoulder by a thin leather strap that wound around the book to keep it closed. But looking back, it was kind of strange for an eight year old boy to carry around such a fancy leather notebook.

I watched him flip open the notebook that day and quickly scribble something onto one of the pages before we walked into the school.

"Oh, I forgot my jacket," I declared and ran back to where I had discarded it by the swings.

I grabbed the jacket and ran to catch up to Drew as he disappeared behind the door of the school. Tugging it open, I expected to see him walking not far ahead, but he wasn't there. I glanced in the nearest classroom. He wasn't in there.

I peeked into the next room and the next and the next. No Drew.

My eyes darted back and forth in the hallway, almost in a panic, scanning the sea of kids filing back into their classes.

Drew was nowhere to be found.

This wasn't the only time he would disappear on me.

As the years passed by, it happened more and more often. I never asked why, and eventually, I stopped looking for him. I was young and impressionable, accepting his disappearances as normal. I wasn't sure where he had gone, but what I knew for sure was that Drew was my best friend and sometimes he was there and sometimes he wasn't.

That seemed to suit our friendship just fine. He would come and go whenever he pleased and I would look forward to every moment with him. It worked. For a while.

But as I got older, I began to wonder. Where did he go? Why didn't he come around my family or friends? When would he show up next? Was he even real? I wanted the answers, but I was too afraid to ask. What if the truth was too strange or scary or out of this world?

My greatest fear was that he would disappear and never come back.